THE GLADIATORS
FROM CAPUA

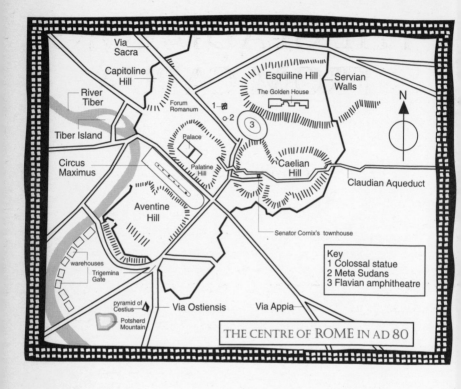

THE CENTRE OF ROME IN AD 80

Via Sacra

Capitoline Hill

River Tiber

Tiber Island

Circus Maximus

Forum Romanum

Palace

Palatine Hill

Aventine Hill

warehouses

Trigemina Gate

pyramid of Cestius

Potsherd Mountain

Via Ostiensis

Esquiline Hill

The Golden House

Servian Walls

N

Caelian Hill

Claudian Aqueduct

Senator Cornix's townhouse

Via Appia

1
2
3

Key
1 Colossal statue
2 Meta Sudans
3 Flavian amphitheatre

— A Roman Mystery —

THE GLADIATORS
FROM CAPUA

Caroline Lawrence

Orion
Children's Books

First published in Great Britain in 2004
by Orion Children's Books
a division of the Orion Publishing Group Ltd
Orion House
5 Upper St Martin's Lane
London WC2H 9EA

Copyright © Roman Mysteries Ltd 2004
Maps by Richard Russell Lawrence
© Orion Children's Books 2004

A catalogue record for this book is
available from the British Library.

ISBN 1 84255 252 X

Printed in Great Britain by Clays Ltd, St Ives plc

To Professor Kathleen Coleman
and the boys of Prince Edward School, Harare

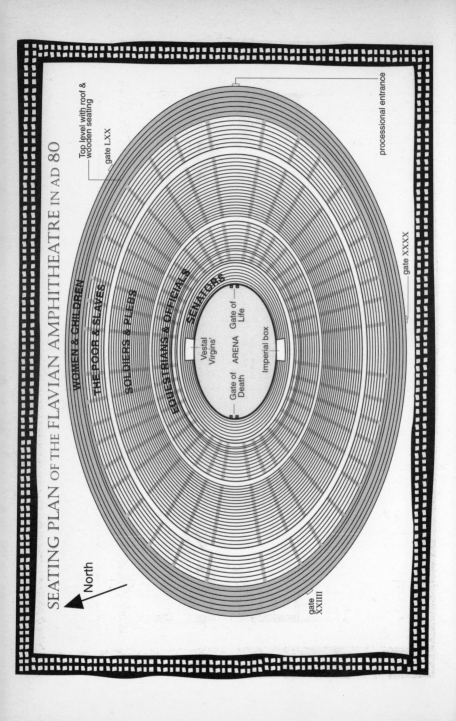

SEATING PLAN OF THE FLAVIAN AMPHITHEATRE IN AD 80

North

WOMEN & CHILDREN

THE POOR & SLAVES

SOLDIERS & PLEBS

EQUESTRIANS & OFFICIALS

SENATORS

Top level with roof &
wooden seating

gate LXX

Vestal
Virgins'

ARENA

Gate of
Life

Gate of
Death

Imperial box

gate XXXX

gate
XXXIIII

processional entrance

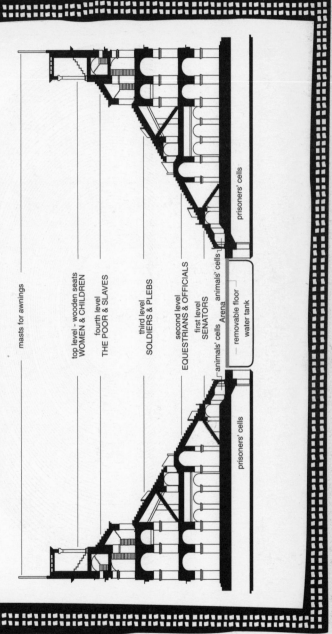

CROSS-SECTION OF
THE FLAVIAN AMPHITHEATRE IN AD 80

masts for awnings

top level - wooden seats
WOMEN & CHILDREN

fourth level
THE POOR & SLAVES

third level
SOLDIERS & PLEBS

second level
EQUESTRIANS & OFFICIALS

first level
SENATORS

Arena

animals' cells

animals' cells

removable floor

water tank

prisoners' cells

prisoners' cells

This story takes place in Ancient Roman times, so a few of the words may look strange.

If you don't know them, 'Aristo's Scroll' at the back of the book will tell you what they mean and how to pronounce them. It will also tell you about some of the different types of gladiators that appear in this book.

SCROLL I

The young gladiator stands on the hot sand and presses the blade of his dagger against his opponent's throat. The secutor is kneeling. His left arm hangs uselessly by his side, broken. His right arm is red, coated with blood from the three-pronged puncture of a trident. The net that brought him down still entangles his feet and behind the small holes of the helmet his eyes roll on terror.

This will be the retiarius's first kill.

Severus the lanista stands nearby. He is watching carefully.

'My men were performing for Nero once,' he says, in a conversational tone. 'One of them, a murmillo, couldn't cut his opponent's throat, although the Emperor demanded it. It was his first kill and he couldn't do it. Nero was so angry that he threw my men to the beasts. All of them. Thirty-two trained gladiators, including Pulcher, only one fight away from winning the wooden sword and his freedom. That,' says Severus, 'is why I always make sure my men can kill before I send them into the arena.'

The retiarius nods, takes a deep breath and shifts the dagger, but he still does not pull it across. From behind the helmet comes a muffled sound. The secutor is whimpering like a wounded animal.

At this moment the retiarius remembers the first time he killed a living creature. The new bow and arrow had been a present for his eighth birthday. He had gone hunting with his father and had shot a young badger. But it hadn't died immediately. It had run in circles – bleeding on the ground in front of him, whimpering pathetically. The retiarius recalls the horror he felt at having caused a living creature such pain and how he wanted to cradle it in his hands and nurse it back to health. 'Father, make it stop. Please make it stop.'

'Crybaby!' The slap had been enough to make his ears ring for hours. But from that day, his father let him tend the goats and never made him hunt again.

Not many years later the Romans came. Some members of his family were killed. Others were sold as slaves.

And he ended up here.

'Being a gladiator is your best chance at freedom,' Severus is saying. 'Freedom with fame and riches. You're good. You could do it. But you can't be a gladiator unless you can kill.'

The retiarius looks down at the knife in his hand. All he has to do is pull it across the throbbing neck. One swift motion.

'Kill him! Kill him!' chant his fellow-gladiators, some encouraging, some jeering.

Severus speaks again and his voice is no longer calm. 'For Jupiter's sake, just do it, man! I've left his helmet on. You don't even have to look him in the face. If you don't kill him, then I swear I'll sell you to the first person who bids for you.'

But the secutor is still whimpering like a wounded animal. The young retiarius shakes his head and tosses his dagger away. His knees crack as he stands up.

'Don't like killing things,' he says. 'Hate blood.'

The man on his knees sobs with relief.

'You idiot!' shouts Severus. 'You're throwing away a glorious future! By all the gods, you're an utter blockhead!'

'I'd rather be a blockhead than a killer,' says the retiarius slowly.

And he walks out of the arena.

Outside the town walls of Ostia, a dark-skinned girl named Nubia laid a wreath of spring wildflowers on the tomb of her friend Jonathan.

It was not a proper tomb because there was no body. Jonathan had died in the terrible fire in Rome a month before and his body was buried in a mass grave with hundreds of others.

Back home in Ostia, the port of Rome, Jonathan's father had paid a stonemason to inscribe Jonathan's name on the family tomb. But it was with other Jewish tombs on the Isola Sacra, almost three miles away.

Nubia and her friends wanted Jonathan's memorial to be closer.

That was why they had crept out one moonlit night to take a disused marble block from beside Ostia's synagogue. The sun was rising by the time they eased the heavy stone off the borrowed handcart.

Now – a week later – Nubia studied the inscription which Flavia had painted on the side of the cracked cube of marble:

D M

IONATANO B. MORDECAE

FLAVIA ET NVBIA ET LVPVS

AMICI AMICO BENE MERENTI

POSVERVNT

Although it was a bright March morning, Nubia shivered and pulled her lionskin cloak closer round her shoulders. She knew DM stood for *dis manibus*: 'to the spirits of the underworld'. The rest meant: 'To Jonathan, son of Mordecai. His friends Flavia, Nubia and Lupus set this up for him, their well-deserving friend.'

There was also a portrait on the tomb, painted by Lupus, who had disappeared shortly afterwards. It wasn't unusual for Lupus to go missing. What was unusual was that a week had passed and he still hadn't returned.

Nubia pushed away her worries about Lupus and focused on the portrait of Jonathan.

It showed a good-looking boy with a square face, olive skin and curly black hair. Lupus had dabbed a tiny dot of white paint on each of the dark eyes to make them really look alive. They really seemed to look straight back at Nubia.

'It's time to say the eulogy,' said Flavia Gemina, and she unrolled a piece of papyrus.

Nubia looked at her former mistress and waited. Flavia was almost eleven years old, with light brown hair and grey eyes. She was not beautiful, but her personality made people forget that. At her best, Flavia was brilliant, confident, and brave. At her worst she was bossy, impetuous and selfish. But she was also kind-hearted. She had bought Nubia to save her from a fate worse than death, then set her free within months.

'Jonathan ben Mordecai,' Flavia began to read in her clear voice, 'was our friend. He was funny and he liked honey. He had asthma and he knew all the psalms by heart. He was good at hunting and very brave and once

4

he saved me from a pack of wild dogs that had me trapped up a tree.' Flavia gestured dramatically with her left arm. 'It was that very oak at the edge of this grove.' She looked at Nubia and the three dogs who sat panting quietly at their feet. 'I thought it fitting that his tomb should lie within sight of that tree: one of his great heroic moments.'

Nubia nodded solemnly and Flavia's dog Scuto thumped his tail.

'On the one hand,' continued Flavia, returning to her scroll, 'Jonathan was a realist. He saw the dark side of life and sometimes it depressed him. But on the other hand, he was very positive. When he discovered that his mother might not have died in the siege of Jerusalem, and that she might be a slave in the Imperial Palace, he bravely went to Rome to search for her. And he succeeded. He found her and he saved her. But he never saw the fruits of his bravery ...'

There was a pause and Nubia saw tears welling in her friend's eyes.

'You never saw what you dreamed of,' Flavia whispered to the portrait on the marble block. 'You never knew the joy of seeing your father and your mother reunited. And, oh Jonathan! You should have seen it when Miriam and your mother fell into each other's arms and they wept and laughed and wept again and went into the garden and talked for hours and hours. And it would all be so perfect if only you hadn't died ...' Flavia's voice was caught by a sob.

Presently she mastered her emotions. 'Now,' she intoned, 'we have come to say goodbye to you, Jonathan. Your father and mother aren't here, because they don't know about this tomb. And Miriam has gone back home. And Lupus disappeared last week; we don't know why. But Nubia and I have come to say farewell.'

'Also the dogs,' said Nubia.

'Also the dogs,' said Flavia, and added: 'Nubia will go first.'

Nubia shook her head. 'Tigris will go first. He has told me what to say ...'

Flavia's grey eyes opened in surprise, but she only nodded.

Nubia looked down at Tigris and put her hand lightly on his head. The big black puppy looked up at her, panting quietly, then looked back towards the little tomb.

Presently Nubia spoke.

'Where are you, master?' said Nubia quietly. 'You told me to stay and to be good dog and I have tried. I am not chewing your father's favourite boot any more. I am not stealing food from the kitchen any more. I am always doing latrine in the garden and not in the study now. So why do you not come?' Nubia took a deep breath and continued. 'Every day I am sitting in the atrium waiting for you with my head on my paws. Whenever I hear someone coming down the street I am putting my ears up to listen very much. But I do not do barking because it is never your footsteps. You are not coming and I miss you. And I am always wondering: Do you not come home because I was a bad dog?'

'Oh Tigris!' cried Flavia. She fell on her knees before the big puppy and threw her arms round his neck. 'It wasn't your fault, Tigris! Jonathan loved you more than anything in the world. You're a good dog.'

Tigris gave a tentative wag of his tail, then whined and

gazed at the tomb.

Presently Flavia stood up and wiped her cheeks with her hand. 'Your turn, now, Nubia,' she said at last.

'Dear Jonathan,' said Nubia to the tomb, 'it is me Nubia speaking to you. I hope you are happy in your paradise which you told me once is like the Land of Green. Thank you for being kind to me when I first came here to Ostia. Thank you for teaching me Latin by reading to me the *Aeneid*. Thank you for making me laugh. I will miss you every day of my life, Jonathon ben Mordecai. Farewell. She bowed her head for a moment and then nodded at Flavia.

Flavia looked down at her sheet of papyrus. For a moment she stared at the words there. Then she rolled it up and slid it into the cord belt of her tunic.

'Jonathan,' she whispered. 'I can't believe you're really dead. I wish we had never gone to Rome. It was my fault. I wanted to solve the Emperor's mystery. The prophecy: "When a Prometheus opens a Pandora's box, Rome will be devastated ..." I thought the prophecy was about the plague getting worse. I should have known it would be about a fire, because Prometheus brought fire down to mankind. And if I'd realised there was going to be a fire maybe you wouldn't have died in it. And maybe you bravely died trying to stop Prometheus but we'll never know because now you're gone and the last time I saw you we argued and I'm so, so sorry. It's my fault you're dead ... I'm sorry Jonathan ...' Flavia sank down before the tomb and laid her head on it. She was weeping. Nubia moved forward, crouched down and put an arm round her friend's shoulders. Her own cheeks were wet, too. All three dogs whined, and Scuto placed a comforting paw on Flavia's arm.

Presently Nubia stood again and took her flute out from beneath her tunic. It always hung on a cord round her neck, close to her heart. As she began to play, the three dogs stopped whining and settled down, resting their chins on their paws.

Each of the holes on Nubia's flute represented a member of her family: the family she had lost the night the slave-traders came.

There was no hole for Jonathan so she made the song his. It was a slow song, and sad. She played it softly with the deepest notes. In her mind she called it 'Lament for Jonathan'. She played the dark green woods on a summer's day, and Jonathan hunting for something he had lost. The notes dripped like warm honey from her flute and, like Flavia, she wept.

Suddenly Nipur barked and the spell was broken. Nubia turned and gasped.

A dark-haired boy in a nutmeg-coloured tunic had emerged from the umbrella pines. He was jogging towards them, waving a wax tablet.

'Lupus!' Nubia cried. 'Where have you been?'

Scuto and Nipur bounded towards the boy – barking and wagging – and then romped back around him. A moment later Lupus stood before them, breathing hard.

Because Lupus had no tongue he relied heavily on his wax tablet. He was waving this triumphantly and it wasn't until Flavia caught his wrist and held it steady that Nubia was able to read the words etched in the wax:

JONATHAN IS NOT DEAD.
HE IS ALIVE!

SCROLL II

'Lupus!' cried Flavia angrily. 'If this is some kind of joke –'

Flavia felt Nubia's fingers dig into her arm and glanced at her friend.

'He is not joking,' said Nubia. 'Behold into his eyes.'

Flavia looked back at Lupus. A look of wild hope burned in his eyes.

'Jonathan's alive?' said Flavia.

Lupus nodded. He was wearing one of Jonathan's old brown tunics. Its size and colour made him look small and pale.

'Are you sure?'

The boy's sea-green eyes flickered and he looked away. Then he wrote on his tablet:

ALMOST POSITIVE
I HEARD SOLDIERS TALKING

'Where?' cried Flavia. 'Have you been to Rome?'

Lupus pointed at the ground impatiently, as if to say: Here in Ostia. Then he continued writing, his bronze stylus making sticky noises as he urgently pushed it through the soft beeswax:

THEY SAY A BOY WITH DARK CURLY HAIR

STARTED THE FIRE IN ROME
AND THAT HE IS HIDING
ON POTSHERD MOUNTAIN

'What is potsherd?' asked Nubia.

'Potsherds are broken bits of clay pots and amphoras,' said Flavia, and frowned. 'I've never heard of any Potsherd Mountain. Where is it, Lupus?'

Lupus shrugged and wrote:

SOMEWHERE IN ROME?

'So you don't really know that Jonathan's alive,' said Flavia carefully. 'You've heard a rumour about a boy with dark, curly hair and you just hope it might be Jonathan, even though we saw the charred rings taken from his body.'

Lupus hung his head and nodded.

'Lupus,' said Nubia softly. 'Where have you been? We have been most worried about you.'

Lupus shrugged and looked away.

'Jonathan's father and mother put up a wooden plaque in the forum,' said Flavia, 'asking if anyone had seen a nine-year-old mute boy with dark hair and green eyes. That's you. And they even paid a signwriter to paint a big notice on the outside of their house.'

Lupus stared at her. For a moment interest flickered in his eyes. Then he shrugged.

THEY DON'T REALLY WANT ME he wrote

I'M NOT THEIR SON

'You are maybe not being their son,' said Nubia fiercely, 'but you are like brother to me and Flavia. Do not ever run away again without telling us where you go! That is overweening!'

Lupus and Flavia stared at Nubia in amazement. She had her hands on her hips and her golden eyes were blazing.

Lupus nodded meekly and gave her a sheepish grin. Flavia laughed and Nubia hugged Lupus. He submitted for a brief moment, then squirmed away.

'Come on,' said Flavia, giving Lupus a quick pat on the back. 'Let's go back home. You have to tell Jonathan's parents you're safe. You can move in with us, if you really think they don't want you, but you must apologise to them. It's hard enough for them as it is, having lost their only son.'

Lupus nodded.

Flavia took a deep breath. 'And let's forget this non-sense about Jonathan still being alive,' she said. 'He's dead, and nothing will ever bring him back.'

'Lupus,' said Jonathan's father in his accented voice. 'I know that now Jonathan is ... gone ... you believe that there is nothing to keep you here. But you are wrong. From the first evening you shared bread and salt with us, you have been under the protection of this household. Also, you have become very dear to me. I want you to stay here.'

Lupus lifted his gaze and studied Doctor Mordecai ben Ezra. Jonathan's father was a tall man, with grey-streaked hair and a sharp nose. Although grief had etched new lines in his face, his dark eyes were warm.

'I want you to stay very much,' repeated Mordecai, 'and so does Jonathan's mother.'

Lupus glanced shyly at the beautiful woman sitting next to Mordecai on the striped divan. But Jonathan's mother was not looking at either of them. She was gazing sadly out through the wide study doorway, into the inner garden.

Lupus felt an almost physical blow to his heart. She obviously didn't care about him.

Mordecai must have seen the expression on his face, because he said sharply, 'Susannah.'

'Yes, my husband?' She turned to Mordecai.

'Tell Lupus what we discussed. That we both want him to stay. To live here with us.'

'Yes, of course,' said Susannah. She focused on Lupus and smiled at him. 'We want you to stay.'

She was very beautiful, and there was kindness in her gaze, but now Lupus was certain that she did not really want him. Anguish flooded his being. He didn't matter to her. It took all his self-control to stop sobbing out loud.

Then the anger welled up in his chest.

He didn't need her. He had a mother. A mother who loved him, who really loved him. And as soon as the sailing season began he would take his ship – HIS ship, not anyone else's – and he would sail back to his own mother and he would never, ever come back to this place.

He lowered his head so that they would not see the emotion he knew must be visible in his eyes and he opened his wax tablet and began to write.

His hand was trembling. They must not know how he felt or they would make him stay and pretend to convince him that they wanted him. And that would be unbearable. So in order to stop his hand shaking, he bit his lip hard.

THANK YOU

he wrote

BUT I THINK I WILL
STAY WITH FLAVIA
FOR A WHILE

He handed the tablet to Mordecai and tried to smile and stood and went into the inner garden and took the leash from its peg and jingled it to summon Tigris for his walk. Somehow he managed to open the back door with trembling hands and to follow Jonathan's dog out into the graveyard.

And when he was finally deep in Diana's grove, Lupus opened his tongueless mouth and howled.

Flavia couldn't sleep.

She stared up at the slanting roof beams and the shadows between them, cast by the steady flame of a tiny bronze oil lamp on her bedside table.

Lupus had come to them late in the afternoon, carrying his few belongings in Jonathan's old leather satchel. They had welcomed him with his favourite dinner of oysters and hardboiled quails' eggs, and later they had made up a bed for him in Aristo's room.

Flavia was worried about Lupus, but the main thing keeping her from sleep was the rumour he had passed on earlier that day. The rumour that a boy with dark, curly hair had started the fire in Rome. And that he was still alive.

She had heard the rumour about the curly-haired boy before. Last month. From the Emperor's astrologer. It was ridiculous that Jonathan could have started the fire, but was there any chance at all that he could still be alive? She rolled onto her right side and considered the possibilities.

They had not seen his actual body, but they had seen his rings, taken from a badly charred corpse. But what if the rings had not come from Jonathan's body? What if he had given all his rings to someone else? Perhaps to get money to buy food? Or for the fare home to Ostia? And then that person had died in the fire?

But no. The man who had given Lupus the rings – a priest from the sanctuary – had said they were taken from a boy's body. It was very unlikely that a boy would have enough money to pay for the rings. An adult, yes. But not a boy of eleven or twelve.

Flavia rolled onto her left side and wormed her feet under Scuto's warm body.

And yet ...

They had never actually *seen* the body.

And what if the priest had been lying? What if Jonathan *was* still alive in Rome, hiding for some reason? Or being kept as a prisoner?

No, no, no. It was ridiculous.

There was no way Jonathan could still be alive. It was just wishful thinking.

Flavia turned to lie on her back again.

'Nubia?' she said very softly. 'Are you awake?'

'Yes.' The reply was instant.

'I know you hate Rome, but if I go back – to try to find Jonathan – will you come with me?'

'Yes,' said Nubia. 'I will go.'

SCROLL III

A. *Caecilius Cornix to M. Flavius Geminus.*

Greetings. I know that I have never corresponded with you before and therefore take this opportunity to apologise. I'm afraid my wife has borne a grudge against you for too long. I have not asked why; women are fickle creatures. I do know for a fact that your daughter did me a great service last month when she came to stay with us. My family – and indeed I myself – were at the Gates of Tartarus when she arrived with several friends, including a certain doctor Mordicus who put us all back on our feet.

While your daughter was staying with us, I promised to invite her back for the inaugural games of the new amphitheatre, which people here in Rome call the eighth wonder of the world. As you know, our illustrious Emperor Titus has decreed a holiday and will open the amphitheatre with one hundred days of spectacles, including gladiatorial contests and beast fights.

I would like to invite Flavia and her friends to stay here at our Rome townhouse for the opening days of this historic occasion.

You are invited, too, of course, though I believe my niece said you were very busy preparing for the sailing season and might be unable to attend. My family and I will be going to Tuscany after the first day of the games; the thought of Rome on holiday for three months is a grim prospect to me. But I shall leave some slaves, including a cook. Your daughter and her friends are most welcome to make use of them and of my house. I look forward to your reply and hope this invitation will *go some way in repairing the rift between our families. Your acceptance will assure me that our families are once more on cordial terms. Goodbye.*

Thank you Sisyphus, thought Flavia, looking up from the letter. I'm glad you're our friend as well as Uncle Cornix's secretary. To her father she said. 'May we go, pater? Please?'

Marcus Flavius Geminus sat back in his leather arm-chair and smiled. He looked thin and tired, and although he was quite old – he would be thirty-two in May – Flavia still thought him handsome.

'I'm not sure,' he said, running a hand through his light brown hair. 'The plague might flare up again. Or there might be another fire. Or you might find another mystery and nearly get yourself killed!'

'But pater, it's an historic event! One I can tell my grandchildren about,' she added pointedly. She knew her father longed for descendants.

'I suppose you could miss a week of lessons,' he said slowly. 'That would free up Aristo to help me prepare the ship for next month.' He narrowed his eyes thoughtfully at her.

Flavia sat up straight on her stool, waiting attentively for his answer.

'Very well,' he said at last, and tried not to smile as she squealed with delight. He held up his hand to ward off her embrace for a moment. 'But you must take Caudex with you as a bodyguard, and you must promise not to get yourself killed.'

Two days later, Flavia Gemina and her friends took an early morning carruca from Ostia to Rome. It was an hour before noon when they arrived at Senator Cornix's Roman townhouse.

Flavia stepped out of the morning sunshine into the shade of a columned porch. 'Dear Castor and Pollux,' she prayed, 'thank you for bringing us safely here.' She glanced over her shoulder at Nubia, Lupus, Tigris and the big door-slave Caudex, still standing in the sunlight. She hadn't told her bodyguard the real reason for the visit so as she turned back to the door she murmured under her breath, 'Please help us find Jonathan if he is still alive.'

As she banged the bronze knocker she added, almost as an afterthought, 'And please, god of Jonathan, will you help us, too?'

'Miss Flavia,' said the dark-eyed Greek with a grin, 'I can't tell you how glad I am to see you! Rome has been so *dull* since you left. And you said in your letter there might be another mystery for us to solve?'

'Of course!' Flavia stepped into the atrium and hugged her uncle's secretary. 'It's so good to see you, Sisyphus! Thanks for getting us invited here.'

'Shhh! The master thinks it was his idea!' Sisyphus peered over Flavia's shoulder: 'Hello Nubia, Lupus, Caudex! Come in.' Then he stiffened. 'Flavia!' he hissed, 'what's that dog doing here? You know Senator Cornix detests dogs.'

'Tigris is very well-behaved,' said Flavia. 'He never even barks these days.' She lowered her voice. 'Sisyphus, there's a chance Jonathan might still be alive, and living here in Rome.'

The Greek's dark eyes grew wide. 'That's your mystery?'

'Yes,' whispered Flavia, 'and if Jonathan *is* alive, we

need Tigris to find his scent.'

'Flavia!' A little girl had run into the atrium. She squealed with delight and threw her arms round Flavia's knees.

'Rhoda!' Flavia laughed and hugged her cousin. Rhoda was four years old and since her two younger sisters had died the previous month, she was once more the baby of the family.

'Nubia!' cried Rhoda, pushing between Flavia and Sisyphus and running out into the porch. Then she stopped still. 'A doggy!' breathed Rhoda reverently. 'Oh Sisyphus, look: a doggy!'

'Come on, then!' Sisyphus grinned and rolled his eyes. 'Let's get you and the mutt installed before Lady Cynthia returns from her friend's house.'

'Thank you, Aunt Cynthia and Uncle Aulus,' said Flavia. 'Thank you for inviting us to stay with you so that we can see the games.'

It was almost midday and they were sitting at a table in a sunny inner courtyard.

'I just wish we could remain here with you ...' Cynthia – an attractive dark-haired woman in her early thirties – glanced up from her wax tablet and gave her husband a pointed look. At the other end of the table Senator Aulus kept his eyes on the scroll he was reading.

Cynthia sighed. 'Don't strangle Flavia, dear,' she said mildly to her youngest child. Rhoda was sitting on Flavia's lap with her arms wrapped round her neck.

The senator sighed, too, as he rolled up his scroll. 'Imagine!' He looked up at them. 'One hundred days of spectacles. No Senate or state business for over three months! The Emperor is –' He stopped and although he was in his own home he lowered his voice, 'Titus has been most irresponsible. Ten days, yes. Even thirty. But one hundred? It's too much!'

'But don't you want to see the games?' asked Flavia. 'You're a senator. You can go every day.'

'The great philosopher Seneca said: "Don't attend the games. Either you'll be corrupted by the masses or – if you remain aloof – be hated by them." We men of noble character despise such spectacles. They are for the plebs. The common people.' He heaved another deep sigh. 'But it is the common people who keep Rome running. And if they all go to the games, this city will grind to a halt.'

'But a million people live here in Rome,' said Flavia's aunt, 'and the new amphitheatre only seats fifty thousand people. Surely they won't all –'

Her husband interrupted her. 'Don't forget about the events at the Stagnum,' he said. 'If the plebs aren't at the new arena they'll all be over there. They'll devour meat from the sacrifices and collect their free grain and watch their mock sea battles and gladiator combats. And in the end they'll forget that the first months of Titus's reign were marked by a volcano, a plague and a fire. It will be a holiday for them. But for us patricians it is so tedious.'

'But you'll attend the opening day, won't you?' asked Flavia, her arms still around Rhoda.

'We really have no choice.' Senator Cornix sighed deeply. 'These are the first games to be sponsored by our new emperor. Titus will be showing Rome his capabilities, character and political agenda through these spectacles.'

'I am not understanding him,' whispered Nubia.

Flavia shifted Rhoda on her lap and leaned towards Nubia. 'He said the games are a big "I'm-the-new emperor" party. If we don't go, we'll hurt Titus's feelings.'

'Oh.'

In the distance Flavia heard the noon gongs announcing the opening of the public baths.

'Excuse me, my dear,' said the senator to his wife. He rose to his feet and adjusted his toga. 'I promised Gnaeus that I'd meet him at the baths. Dinner as usual?'

'Yes, dear.'

'Sisyphus, I need you to come and take dictation on the way.' The senator strode off towards the front of the house. Sisyphus gave Flavia a mock sigh and hurried after him.

'I want to go to the games, too,' said Rhoda. 'I want to go to the games with Flavia and Nubia and Lupus and the doggy.'

Flavia kissed the top of Rhoda's head. The little girl had light brown hair, the same colour as her own. 'Aunt Cynthia, have you ever heard of something called Potsherd Mountain?'

'I have,' said a boy, coming into the bright courtyard.

'Hello, Aulus!' said Flavia. 'How are you?'

He shrugged. 'Hello, everybody.'

'Hello, Aulus,' said Nubia, and Lupus waved.

'Are your lessons finished for the day, dear?' asked Cynthia.

'Obviously.' Aulus slumped onto the bench next to Lupus and reached under the table to give Tigris a scratch behind the ear. 'Potsherd Mountain,' he said to Flavia, 'is a hill made of broken pots and amphoras. It's over beyond the Aventine, outside the city walls between the river and the pyramid.'

'I didn't know that,' said Cynthia, putting down her stylus. 'How did you know that, dear?'

Aulus shrugged. 'Everybody knows it,' he said, and looked at Flavia. 'Would you like to see it?'

'We want to see it! We want to see it!' cried two boys, running into the courtyard. Quintus and Sextus were five-year-old twins with dark hair and bright eyes.

'No. You two can't come,' said Aulus with a yawn. 'And neither can you, Hyacinth.' This last was addressed to a girl of about nine who had stopped by one of the columns which flanked the entry to the courtyard.

'Hello, Hyacinth!' called Flavia. 'Hello, Quintus and Sextus.'

'It's not fair, mater!' cried the twins. 'We want to go, too.'

'I want to go, too!' said Rhoda from Flavia's lap.

'Well, you can't,' said Aulus. 'You have to be nine or older to come.'

'Lupus isn't nine,' said Hyacinth from her column.

'Actually he is,' said Flavia. 'He turned nine last month.'

'I'm going to be nine in May,' said Hyacinth, lifting her chin.

'Well, that's just too late!' Aulus smirked at her.

'Who died and made you emperor?' said Hyacinth. 'Mater, may I go with them?'

'You don't even know where we're going!'

'Potsherd Mountain! Potsherd Mountain!' chanted the twins. 'We want to go! We want to go!'

'Mama!' squealed Rhoda, bouncing up and down on Flavia's lap. 'I want to go, too. Can I be nine?'

Nubia burst into tears.

SCROLL IV

'Are you feeling better now?' asked Flavia, putting her arm around Nubia.

Nubia nodded.

She and Flavia were walking down a steep hill behind Caudex, Aulus, and Lupus. Tigris led the way, stretching the lead in Lupus's hand taut.

Nubia remembered the first time she had seen this street, which Aulus called the Clivus Scauri. She had been riding with Flavia in a litter on a hot summer's evening. Now it was cloudy and grey with a strange wind from the south. The wind moaned through the column-ed porches on either side and rustled the dark tops of the umbrella pines high above. Nubia shivered.

'Are you cold?' asked Flavia.

'No. My lionskin cloak is keeping me warm.'

'Then what's wrong? Why were you crying earlier?'

Nubia tried to find the words. 'I miss my family,' she said at last.

Flavia nodded. 'I forget sometimes how hard it must be for you. Maybe it was a bad idea: us coming to stay with my cousins.'

'No,' said Nubia. 'Your cousins please me: the twins and the little girl Rhoda and the mother like a tall palm tree who sways if the wind beats it but is never broken ... My mother was like that.'

'Oh, Nubia. They remind you of your family. That's why you cried.'

Nubia nodded and tried to swallow the tightness in her throat.

As they reached the foot of the Caelian Hill, Aulus turned left. Although wheeled traffic was not allowed into Rome during the day, some people were boldly driving donkey carts laden with supplies. Tigris strained at his lead with his nose down and Nubia noticed his tail wag now and again. They skirted the southern end of the great Circus Maximus and moved through a crowded shopping district full of people hurrying to buy oil, wine, dried beans and wheat on the last day before the games.

Presently they came into a square so full of people that at first Nubia did not recognize it. But then she saw the three white arches of the Trigemina Gate rising above the crowds. Through those arches lay the road back to Ostia.

She felt the crowd pushing her strongly from behind and tried to ignore the wave of panic rising up in her. She was used to the empty space of the desert, not crowds of smelly, noisy people. Someone's elbow dug into her ribs and a fat man trod on her toe with his hobnailed boots.

'Coming through!' announced a slave in a high nasal voice and the pole of a sedan chair caught Nubia a glancing blow on her cheekbone.

'Watch where you're going!' Flavia shouted angrily and Nubia felt her friend's grip.

'Over here, Nubia,' said Flavia. 'It's safest in Caudex's wake.'

Nubia and Flavia stayed close behind Caudex. He was a big man and the crowds parted before him as they began to move again.

Finally they passed through the gate.

'Behold the pyramid,' said Nubia wistfully, recognizing a landmark on the road back to Ostia. But they did not take the left-hand road, which led to Ostia, and they did not take the right-hand road, which skirted a green hill. Instead, Aulus led them along the middle way. And now Nubia saw what she had never seen before.

Rome had expanded beyond the city walls. Behind the tomb-lined roads were the workshops of potters and blacksmiths. One shop made carts and carriages and another displayed gates and tables of wrought iron.

'Behold the tall brick buildings ahead,' said Nubia, 'like at Ostia.'

'Warehouses,' said Flavia. 'The river must be over there.'

As they moved towards the warehouses, Nubia saw more and more shops had furnaces which blanketed the area with their smoke.

Tigris sneezed, then lifted his nose to test the air.

'There it is,' said Aulus Junior, nodding towards a low hill between some two-storey workshops and the warehouses beyond. 'Potsherd Mountain.'

'That is being Potsherd Mountain?' asked Nubia. She had imagined a towering red cone made of broken pottery so sharp that Jonathan's knees and hands would be bloody from trying to scramble over it. 'It is not a mountain,' she said to Aulus, 'it is just a hill.'

Lupus grunted his agreement.

'And I didn't think it would have grass growing on it,' added Flavia.

'Well, I wasn't the one who named it,' said Aulus.

'And it only takes a season for grass to start growing.'

'Look how they've arranged the pieces neatly into layers,' said Flavia. 'I suppose they'd have landslides if they didn't.'

'Behold!' cried Nubia. 'There's a person up there!'

'Stop saying "Behold!",' snapped Aulus. 'Nobody says that.'

'It's poetic,' said Flavia. 'We like it when Nubia says "Behold!"'

'But it sounds stupid,' said Aulus. 'And she *looks* stupid in that lionskin.'

'What should I say?' asked Nubia in a small voice.

'Just say "look" like any normal person. Uh-oh. Beggars.'

Three men in tattered clothes had appeared and were making for them with hands outstretched. 'Coppers for the poor,' one of them pleaded in a quavering voice.

'Shards for sale,' said another, and Nubia stared in horror: someone had cut off his nose.

Caudex stepped forward to drive the beggars away, but Flavia put a restraining hand on his muscular forearm. Then Nubia saw her reach under her cloak and fish in her coin purse.

'Don't give them anything!' hissed Aulus. 'You'll just encourage them.'

Flavia ignored him. She held up a small silver coin for the beggars to see.

'I'll give this denarius,' she announced in a clear voice, 'to anyone with information about a boy with dark curly hair who lives on that hill.'

The beggars stared at her, then glanced at one another.

'They say,' continued Flavia, 'that he was the one who started the fire last month.'

As one, the beggars turned and fled.

'Are you stupid?' said Aulus to Flavia. 'I thought you just wanted to see Potsherd Mountain, not get us all arrested. Why did you mention the fire? Are you a complete blockhead?'

Flavia stared at him. Beside her, Caudex stiffened.

Aulus rolled his eyes. 'Listen: if they suspect you had anything to do with the fire they'll cart you off to the prison. You know what they do to arsonists, don't you?' He spoke slowly, as if addressing an idiot.

Flavia shook her head.

'They throw them to the beasts.'

Flavia felt a tug at her tunic. She looked away from Aulus's angry face. 'What is it, Lupus?'

Lupus pointed to a narrow alley between two workshops. It was full of rubbish.

'What?' repeated Flavia, looking back down at him.

'Beho – look!' said Nubia. 'There is someone there.'

Then Flavia saw it. The gleam of eyes in a grubby, feral face. It was a boy in a striped skullcap, crouching in the alley and watching them. As their eyes met, the urchin beckoned her with a finger.

Flavia glanced at the others. 'Wait here with Caudex,' she commanded.

Aulus snorted. 'Who died and made you emperor?' he asked.

'Wait here,' she repeated coldly, narrowing her eyes.

Aulus glared back at her but she ignored him and picked her way through the rubbish in the alley. For a moment she thought the beggar had gone. Then a small hand gripped her wrist and pulled her down out of sight, behind some planks of rotten wood and a broken cart-wheel.

'I heard what you asked those men,' whispered the urchin. Flavia could see now that it was not a boy, but a girl who had pushed her hair up into her skullcap. 'A boy has been living on Potsherd Mountain,' said the girl. 'Since the fire.'

Flavia's eyes grew wide. 'A boy with dark curly hair? About eleven years old.'

The beggar-girl nodded.

'Is his name Jonathan?' Flavia's heart was pounding.

The girl shrugged. 'It may have been. They call him Hilarus, because he's funny.'

'Which part of Potsherd Mountain does he live on?'

The girl held out her hand.

'Oh,' said Flavia, and placed a silver denarius in the grubby palm. 'Now tell me: where is he?'

'He's not here any more. He's at the new amphi-theatre. Some soldiers arrested him yesterday morning.' The girl showed sharp little teeth in a smile and then giggled. 'They're going to throw him to the beasts.'

SCROLL V

'So now you're dragging us along to the new amphitheatre?' said Aulus. 'What is this? A tour of Rome?'

Flavia ignored him. 'I wonder,' she mused, 'where they keep the prisoners?'

'Prisoners?' said Aulus. 'Why do you want to know about the prisoners? And what was all that about a boy with dark curly hair?'

Flavia hesitated. She didn't want to tell Aulus the real reason for their quest.

'We're just trying to find out who started the fire last month,' she said.

'You're *what?*'

'We're detectives,' said Flavia. 'We solve mysteries.'

'That's stupid,' said Aulus.

They had just passed the Circus Maximus and were walking with the green Palatine Hill on their left and the brick-red aqueduct straight ahead. Flavia put her hands on her hips and turned to face Aulus. Caudex, Lupus and Nubia stopped, too. Tigris investigated the base of an umbrella pine.

'Our stupid detective work saved the Emperor's life last year,' Flavia said to Aulus. 'And he asked us to solve a mystery for him last month.'

'But you didn't solve the mystery, did you? You never found out who Pygmalion was.'

'Prometheus,' said Flavia, 'we were trying to find a Prometheus. And we still are,' she lied.

Aulus snorted.

'If you think our investigation is stupid,' said Flavia coldly, 'why don't you just go home?'

'I think I will!' he said between clenched teeth. 'I need to pack my things. Because we're leaving the day after tomorrow and that's good. It means I won't have to see you again.'

'That's fine with me.'

'Fine with me, too!' Aulus Junior turned and stalked off towards the Caelian Hill.

Nubia gazed in wonder at the huge amphitheatre before her.

It was immensely tall, with four storeys. The three lower levels were pierced with rows of arched niches framed by half columns. Each niche held a statue or group of statues and each statue was painted, so that it really looked as if a hundred colourful gods and heroes stood in the massive structure and gazed out over Rome.

'Look, Nubia,' said Flavia beside her. 'There are some of the types of columns that Aristo was teaching us about: Tuscan, Ionic and Corinthian at the very top.'

Nubia nodded and tipped her head back.

The plain top storey of the colossal monument was covered with scaffolding and she saw slaves moving about up there. She wasn't sure what they were doing but she heard the sound of hammering drifting down. On the ground were more slaves. Some carried twig brooms or clay pots of paint, some drove carts which arrived full of pale yellow sand and went away empty. Others knotted ropes to marble posts. Nubia's head went back again as she followed the lines up to the very top of the monumental building.

It was impossibly high and vast. Did mere humans really build it? Was Jonathan really alive in there somewhere?

Nubia closed her eyes for a moment and reached out with her intuition, trying to see if she could feel his presence.

Nothing.

So she focused on her other senses. She could smell animals. She could hear an elephant's echoing trumpet from within. And she could feel warm drops falling on her face and arms.

Nubia opened her eyes. And cried out in horror.

It was raining blood.

'Nubia! What's wrong!' cried Flavia Gemina.

Nubia pointed to the reddish brown drops spattering onto her lionskin cloak. 'It is raining with blood!' she cried. 'Blood!'

Flavia laughed. 'It's not blood. It's only rain.'

'But it is even warm like blood!' Nubia made the sign against evil.

'No, no, Nubia! It's only dust in the rain. Sometimes when the wind is from the south it brings red dust. Pater says it's from a great desert across the sea. When it rains, the dust fills the raindrops and it looks like blood.' She rubbed one of the marks on Nubia's cloak. 'See? That will come out easily.'

'It will?' asked Nubia in a small voice.

Flavia nodded. 'Come on, everyone. Let's wait under that tree. This rain doesn't look as if it will last.' She looked up at the grey sky. 'Now that Aulus is gone we can concentrate on finding – Caudex, do you have any idea where they would keep the people they intend to throw to the beasts?'

The big bodyguard stared at her stupidly.

Flavia sighed. 'Caudex,' she said. 'There's a chance – a very small chance – that Jonathan might be alive.'

Caudex's small brown eyes widened. 'But you said ...' he trailed off in confusion.

'I know we said he died in the fire last month and yes – we saw his charred rings. But we never actually saw his body. And there have been rumours that a boy with dark curly hair started the fire and that he was hiding on Potsherd Mountain. But that beggar-girl I was talking to just now said they've taken him to the amphitheatre to throw to the beasts. Caudex, if it's Jonathan we've got to save him. Do you understand?'

Caudex nodded. His big, square jaw was set.

'Caudex, you used to be a gladiator, didn't you?'

He shrugged. 'Never fought,' he mumbled.

'But you *trained*, didn't you?'

He nodded.

'Then tell us. Where would they keep the gladiators before they fight the animals?'

'Gladiators don't fight animals,' said Caudex slowly. 'Gladiators fight other gladiators. Beast-fighters fight beasts. And criminals,' he stopped to think, 'especially the people who set fires –'

'Arsonists,' said Flavia.

Caudex nodded. 'They throw them to the lions.'

'We've got to work fast,' said Flavia to her friends. 'In four hours it will be dark and tomorrow the games begin. I suggest we split up and try to get any information we can. Lupus, you can go almost anywhere without people noticing you. See if you can find where the prisoners are held. Nubia, why don't you find out where the beasts are kept and ask there? Caudex, you trained as a gladiator, so maybe you can pretend to be a gladiator who's lost his way. We'll meet at sunset, over there by the *meta sudans*.' Flavia pointed to a large, wet black marble cone.

They all nodded and then Lupus pointed at Flavia and raised his eyebrows as if to say: What will you do?

'I'm going to spy on that man with the ponytail over there. He seems to be ordering all those slaves around so he must be in charge. He'll know where the convicted criminals are kept. I'll take Tigris with me.' She looked at each one of them. 'Remember: the trick is to act like you belong. I know it's scary, but if the curly-haired boy really is Jonathan then this may be our last chance to save him.'

Lupus had been writing something. Now he tugged Flavia's palla and held up his wax tablet almost apologetically.

WHAT DO WE DO
IF WE FIND HIM?

Flavia stared at the tablet, and then at her friends. They were all gazing at her, waiting for her to tell them what to do. Even Tigris had fixed his liquid brown eyes on Flavia's face and was panting hopefully. She forced herself to smile. 'I'm not sure what we'll do if we find him,' she admitted, 'but I promise you this: I'll think of something!'

SCROLL VI

It had been a long time since Nubia had smelled camel dung.

The scent grew stronger as she moved towards the south side of the huge amphitheatre, and it brought memories rushing back.

One memory was particularly vivid.

The year before, Nubia's family had been travelling in the spring caravan to the Blue Oasis where the annual spice market was held. She and her elder brother Taharqo had been sharing a ride on Nubia's camel. Siwa was named after the famous oasis of date palms, because – like Nubia – he adored dates.

'Siwa!' she would call, and toss a date from where she sat on his high back. The camel would turn his big head and catch the date neatly in his mouth. A moment later he would spit out the stone.

Nubia proudly showed Taharqo this trick. He had been so impressed that he grabbed Nubia's bag of dates.

'No!' cried Nubia and tried to retrieve her dates. But Taharqo held the bag up high, out of her reach.

'Siwa!' he cried, and tossed a date to the camel's right.

Siwa lurched right to catch the flying date. Nubia yelped as she almost fell off the camel's lofty hump.

35

'Siwa!' cried Taharqo and threw a date to the left.

The camel veered left and with a squeal Nubia clutched at her brother to stop herself falling off. The dunes were soft but they were a long way down.

'Siwa!' laughed Taharqo.

'Stop, Taharqo!' But Nubia was laughing, too.

'Siwa!'

Left.

'Siwa!'

Right.

Taharqo was laughing so hard now that his throws were wild and the camel's movement even more violent.

'Siwa!!'

The camel had to make such a violent lunge to catch the tasty morsel that he almost lost his balance. He righted himself at the last moment, but Nubia and Taharqo tumbled off his back and landed on the soft dunes.

Right in a pile of camel dung.

They had still been laughing as Siwa happily devoured the scattered dates around them.

But the whole caravan had been forced to halt and as punishment, Nubia's father refused them permission to change their clothes. They arrived at the Blue Oasis three hours later smelling of camel dung.

Nubia's smile grew broader.

Taharqo had been furious. A girl he liked had taken one sniff and run giggling back to her friends.

Their father had laughed and said the test of true love was the 'camel-dung test'. And Nubia's mother had replied with a solemn face, 'Yes, my husband. And I have passed that test many times.'

Nubia's smile faded and her eyes filled with tears. Her father was dead and her mother, too. Slaughtered by slave-traders. The familiar tightness closed round her throat. Her family would never laugh together like that again.

Lupus rubbed dirt into his hair and over his cheeks, glad that he had worn his plain travelling tunic. Then he watched from behind an umbrella pine. Presently one of the slaves left his twig broom leaning against a wall and disappeared under a marble arch to relieve himself. Darting forward, Lupus snatched the broom. Head down, sweeping as he went, he moved along to another of the arched entrances. Before he entered, he glanced up, just to get his bearings. The Roman numeral XXIIII was incised above it and picked out in red paint. Twenty-four. He was entering the amphitheatre at gate number twenty-four.

Flavia pulled her dove-grey palla over her head; the low clouds were still spitting rain. She allowed Tigris to pull her nearer to the man giving orders, and watched him from behind a cart full of sand. She guessed he was about her father's age, maybe younger. He wore a cream tunic with two dark vertical stripes. His long dark hair was pulled back in a ponytail. Although he was not tall, he gave the impression of absolute authority, giving orders with cheerful abuse or slaps on the back.

When a couple of highborn women walked past he called out: 'Looking for a date with a gladiator, ladies? I can fix you up!'

The two women hurried off with scandalised expressions and Ponytail roared with laughter. Then he whirled and pointed at the cart behind which Flavia was hiding.

'You! Scaevus!' he yelled. 'Get that sand in the arena before it soaks up another ton of rainwater.'

The driver cracked his whip and the cart rolled slowly towards gate number forty. Flavia and Tigris moved along with the cart and at the last minute slipped into the shelter of the arched gateway next to it. From here Flavia was close enough to see that the man with the ponytail had brown eyes and pockmarked skin.

A bald man and two girls of about Flavia's age approached Ponytail, and stood waiting as he signed a wax tablet held by a scribe.

Ponytail turned away from the scribe and looked the girls up and down. 'Water nymphs for the Orpheus routine?' he asked the bald man.

Baldy grunted yes.

'They look the part,' said Ponytail. 'What's your name, darling?' he said to one of the girls. Flavia didn't hear her mumbled reply.

'What are you? About twelve?'

The girl nodded and looked up at Ponytail with solemn blue eyes.

'Freeborn?'

The girl nodded.

'Parents still alive?'

'My mother is.'

'Blastus, you fool!' said Ponytail to the bald man. 'The Emperor's brother wants slaves and orphans. Get me fair-haired girls who are slaves or orphans. Sorry, darling, you'd best run along home.'

The girl burst into tears and ran off.

'What about you?' said Ponytail to the other girl. 'What's your name?'

'Marcia,' said the girl in a clear voice.

'How old?'

'Ten.'

'Parents alive?'

'No. I'm an orphan. I live by myself.'

'Looks like it, too,' said Ponytail. 'But you'll do. By this time on the day after tomorrow you'll have a thousand sesterces in gold coins. Not bad for a few hours' work, is it?' He patted her on the head and turned to Blastus. 'Tell Mater to get her bathed, perfumed and looking beautiful. Then go out and find me one more. I want a nice half dozen.'

'Yes, sir.'

As Blastus and the girl called Marcia walked away, they passed by the arch where Flavia and Tigris were hiding. Marcia was saying something to Blastus, and smiling with sharp little teeth. Flavia pressed herself against the painted stucco wall, her heart beating fast. She had just recognised the blonde. Marcia was the beggar-girl from the foot of Potsherd Mountain.

Nubia stood among a crowd of Romans watching a processional of carts make their way to the processional entrance of the amphitheatre. The carts had been passing for nearly an hour, and she had counted more than fifty exotic beasts go past, among them giraffes, elephants, tigers, bears and lions. Now the crowd gasped as a sloshing cart full of water brought a huge grey creature towards the main entrance.

When Nubia had first arrived the crowd had been

sparse. Now it was big, and getting bigger.

'It's a hippopotamus,' shouted a man. 'A river-horse!'

The crowd surged forward to see it.

'Back!' shouted the man walking beside the cart. 'These creatures are extremely dangerous!'

A few moments later Nubia heard the distinctive jingling stomp of a unit of marching soldiers. They began to take up position in front of the crowds.

Nubia realised she must do something quickly or she would never get into the amphitheatre.

She remembered Flavia's words: *The trick is to act like you belong.*

Taking a deep breath she boldly stepped out of the crowd and fell into step with some slaves walking beside a large wooden cage.

'Hey, you!' she heard someone shout. She stared resolutely ahead, resisting the temptation to panic and run away.

'Hey, you!' came the voice again. 'Hercula! You going to wrestle that lion with your bare hands?'

Laughter.

Nubia sighed a secret sigh of relief. It was just her cloak that was attracting attention: a lionskin cloak like the one the mythical hero Hercules wore. She glanced up at the cage beside her. She was too low to see the animal through the small barred window at the top but she could smell lion.

Suddenly she gasped as an iron grip closed round her wrist.

'Sorry, miss,' said the soldier sternly. 'But I'm afraid you'll have to come with me.'

SCROLL VII

Lupus moved further into the great amphitheatre, sweeping as he went.

Once, two workmen passed by. One held thick ropes of flowers and the other pots of paint. Neither of them took any notice of the lowly slave-boy sweeping the corridors.

The further in he went on this level the darker it became. Here the corridors were lit by flickering torches in wall brackets. It occurred to Lupus that if these torches went out a person might wander in the maze forever.

Now he was alone. He had not met anyone for five or ten minutes and he only had the brisk sound of his twig broom to keep away the fear and the ghosts.

Suddenly he stopped sweeping. Drifting out from the dark mouth of the corridor up ahead was an eerie wailing noise. Lupus felt the short hair on the back of his neck stand right up, just as he had seen the hackles rise on the back of a dog.

He had never in his life felt such a clear premonition of horror as he did now. And so he did the only sensible thing.

Lupus dropped his broom, turned and ran.

'You'd better come away from there!' said the soldier to Nubia. 'Unless you're with this lion.'

'Of course she's with this lion,' said a man's accented voice behind Nubia. 'Can't you see she's wearing his father's skin?'

'Mnason!' cried Nubia in delight. She knew the Syrian animal trainer from Ostia; she had helped him recapture an escaped lion and giraffe.

The soldier shrugged and released Nubia's wrist. 'Just trying to keep some order,' he growled, and clinked off along the line of carts.

'Nubia! What a delightful surprise!' said Mnason, when the soldier was out of earshot. 'And I'm glad to see you're wearing the cloak I gave you.'

'It pleases me. It is keeping me warm. Is the Monobaz here?'

Mnason nodded and jerked his thumb towards the cart behind. 'Right back there ...'

'He is well?'

Mnason fell into step with her and they walked beside the slowly-moving cart. 'He is in peak form, my dear. In peak form. In fact he is on tomorrow's programme.'

'Is that good?'

'To be on the first and greatest day of the games? I should say so.'

'He will not be eating people, will he?' asked Nubia in a small voice.

'Of course not!' laughed Mnason. 'He's a trick lion, not a common man-eater. Just you wait and see.'

At last the cart was entering the special gate beneath the marble sculpture of a four-horse chariot.

Nubia hesitated.

'Are you coming in?'

'Yes,' she said, taking a deep breath. 'I am coming with you and the Monobaz.'

'Excuse me, young lady.'

Flavia jumped. A thin man holding several pieces of papyrus stood behind her. He looked down at Tigris who was panting softly.

'Just taking your dog for a walk?' he asked mildly. He was obviously a scribe or clerk.

'Um, yes.'

'Well, you look like a highborn girl, so let me offer you a piece of advice. Don't loiter here under the arches. It's where the women in togas ply their trade. You might get ... unwelcome attention.'

'Oh. Thank you. My dog and I were just leaving.' Flavia gave Tigris's lead a little tug, and as she walked out from under the archway, the thin man consulted his wax tablet and hurried after her.

'Wait! Before you go ... I'm looking for the organiser, Quintus Fabius Balbus. That man over there with the ponytail ... would he be the *magister ludi*?'

Flavia looked at Ponytail. 'Yes,' she said, and looked at the scribe. 'I think that must be the *magister ludi*.'

Lupus smiled sheepishly.

What a coward he was! He was deep in the bowels of a vast monument devoted to violent death, looking for condemned criminals. What did he expect to hear? Jolly choruses?

He took a deep breath, turned and forced himself to move back through the corridors. Back the way he had come. Back towards the eerie wailing noise.

SCROLL VIII

Lupus found his broom where he had dropped it. He picked it up and gazed unhappily at the three dark corridors before him. He had no idea which one to take. The eerie noise had ceased and he could only hear the crackling flames of the wall torches. He closed his eyes and rested his forehead against the wooden broom handle and prayed.

'You there! Stop leaning on your broom and give me a hand.'

Lupus started. A slave in a pale tunic was glaring at him.

'Take one of these buckets,' ordered the slave. He had an enormous wart on his right eyelid which gave him an unpleasant leer. 'Come on! I don't have all day. It's feeding time for the prisoners.'

Lupus dropped his broom and ran to take one of the wooden pails from the big slave. It was full of water and he could see a copper beaker lying at the bottom. The big slave shifted his remaining pail to the other hand and adjusted the bulging canvas shoulder bag slung over one shoulder. Then he strode off down the middle corridor.

'Fungus was supposed to help me,' he said over his shoulder, 'but he never does his share. Always playing dice with Pupienus. Come on, boy! Keep up. And try not to spill any water: it makes the floor muddy.'

Mnason let out his breath in a slow whistle. 'Look at this cell,' he said. 'Bright, well-ventilated, a constantly replenished water trough, fresh hay on the ground. See this, Monobaz?'

Monobaz emerged blinking from his wooden cage, padded down the ramp and sniffed the hay. Then he flopped onto his side.

'Nothing but the best for my kitty.' Mnason scratched Monobaz behind the ear and the big cat's whole body vibrated with a rhythmic purring.

'I wonder where they are keeping the prisoners,' said Nubia, looking around.

'Well, if their cells are half as nice as these, they won't want to leave, will they, Monobaz?'

Lupus followed Verucus into a dim vaulted room, and nearly gagged at the powerful stench of human sweat and excrement. Behind a second barrier of iron bars, more than two hundred faces turned towards him as the door slammed shut. The prisoners – almost all of them bearded men – sat on the beaten earth floor. The only person standing was a short man with a turban, who had obviously been addressing the criminals.

Lupus saw that the man wore a black and white shawl over his shoulders. He had seen a rabbi at Jonathan's synagogue wearing such a shawl.

Lupus braced himself for the stampede Verucus had predicted, but the people remained seating.

'Good,' said the rabbi to them in accented Latin. 'That is good. No panic. No wailing. Now. We will pass the bread to the younger boys first. Then us men.

And I want two of you –' he gazed round, then pointed, '– you, Reuben ... and you, Shmuel ... get the water and ladle it out. Remember,' the rabbi was telling the prisoners, 'the Master of the Universe – blessed be he – is watching us. We have a chance to please him in the last hours of our lives. How many people get such an opportunity?'

As the two bearded men picked their way carefully through the seated crowd towards the bars, Lupus quickly scanned the prisoners for his friend. His heart thumped several times, for there were a surprising number of heads with dark curly hair, but none of them was Jonathan.

Verucus was taking leathery discs out of his canvas shoulder bag and passing them through the bars to eager hands. As the bread was passed along to those most in need, the rabbi began to intone something in another language. Lupus instantly recognised the first few words of the Hebrew blessing that Jonathan's father recited every day over the food: '*Barooch ata adonai elohay noo melech ha olam ...*'

Lupus felt as if he had been kicked in the stomach. He suddenly realised who the prisoners were. They were all Jews.

'Well,' said Mnason to Nubia. 'I'll ask around, but the prisoners are in a different part of the amphitheatre. I've heard there are some cells on the west side ...'

'Father!' said a youth of about fourteen. He had Mnason's black hair and olive skin, but his cheeks were smooth. 'Come quickly! The gladiators are about to rehearse their procession into the arena.'

Mnason looked up from brushing Monobaz's golden fur. 'Nubia, this is my son, Bar-Mnason. We call him Bar for short.'

Bar looked Nubia up and down, then grinned.

Mnason pulled off one of his necklaces – a stamped clay tag on a leather thong – and handed it to Nubia. 'Here,' he said. 'Take this. It's a pass to the beast-keepers' area. If anybody asks what you're doing just say you're with Mnason's group. Now run along with Bar to see the gladiators. You can help me feed Monobaz later.'

'Hey, you! What are you doing here? This area is strictly off-limits.'

'I'm sorry, sir,' lisped Flavia in her little girl's voice, 'but my doggy ran in and I'm just going to get him.' Flavia pointed at Tigris, waiting patiently at the top of the stairs inside an arch of the amphitheatre.

The guard narrowed his eyes at her.

By thinking about Jonathan, Flavia managed to fill her eyes with tears. She also let her chin quiver.

'Oh, all right! But be quick about it. No loitering!'

'Yes, sir. Thank you, sir.'

Flavia sighed. She wouldn't be able to use the little girl ploy much longer. She took the marble steps two at a time, picked up Tigris's lead and together they moved deeper into the structure. Presently the puppy led her into a bright, honey-scented space with big colourful columns and a low marble parapet.

The sweet smell came from garlands of spring flowers draped from the tops of the columns before her. Pink peony, yellow narcissus, and purple crocus were twined with creamy honeysuckle. The same colours that swirled through the marble of the polished columns.

Flavia moved forward to see the whole amphitheatre framed between these columns.

She gasped.

It was enormous.

Its walls were tier upon tier of marble seating rising up and away from her. Its floor was a huge oval of pale sand and its ceiling was a red awning high above the amphitheatre. Even as she craned her neck to look up she saw a lofty square of red fold itself up, seemingly without human help. There was a hint of blue between the thinning clouds that promised good weather for the following day.

Looking around, Flavia saw that she stood in the lowest tier of the great amphitheatre and suddenly realised she must be in the Imperial Box. Tomorrow the Emperor himself would sit here.

Slaves hovered over the seats on either side, dipping paintbrushes into clay pots and applying them to the marble benches that curved around the vast seating area. Flavia looked down on one of these slaves, and saw that he was filling the inscribed seat numbers with red paint to make them easily legible. He also picked out the lines dividing one seat space from the next.

Abruptly Flavia froze. A strange moaning sound filled the amphitheatre. It sounded like a giant's groan.

The noise seemed to come from an object at one end of the arena on the lowest level of seats. It was a big wooden box with copper sticks poking up from it, each a different length. The copper sticks reminded Flavia of upside-down pan-pipes and she realised it was exactly that: an instrument with giant bronze pipes.

A man stood behind this box and two slaves crouched on either side. Although the man was not blowing he was doing something to the box to make it breathe. Now the sound was lighter, higher, as if the giant was humming. The sound made her heart beat fast and her stomach sink, as if something exciting was about to happen.

She saw that many of the slaves had stopped to look, too, and from the unseen tier above her head she heard a man yell: 'Get back to work, you lot!'

As Flavia stood listening to the compelling sound of the strange instrument, she saw two people appear on the far side of the arena at her level. Flavia squinted. One was a dark-skinned figure in a tawny cloak.

Flavia waved at Nubia, and her friend waved back. Flavia shook her head slowly and gave an exaggerated shrug, to let her know she hadn't discovered anything yet.

Across the arena, Nubia saw Flavia shake her head and shrug. She nodded, to show she'd understood, then pointed at herself and shook her head too.

'Do you know that person over there?' Bar asked Nubia in surprise.

She nodded. 'That is my friend Flavia Gemina. What is the noise?'

'The water organ? Haven't you heard one of those before? Strange, isn't it?'

'I like it.'

'Me, too. Father says it just stirs up the crowd, but I think it makes the games more exciting.'

The water organ played another sequence of dramatic chords. Suddenly trumpets blared out a fanfare and

Nubia saw two men in togas emerge from an arched gate below the water organ. They were carrying strange bundles of something like twigs. Three men blowing large curved trumpets strutted after them into the bright arena. And then came the men.

'Here they come,' said Bar. 'Here come the gladiators.'

SCROLL IX

As the forerunners of the procession marched out into the arena, Nubia saw a slave who had been raking sand stop and stare, then scamper off.

A moment later a man with a ponytail come into sight on the sandy oval of the arena below them.

'That's Fabius,' remarked Bar. 'He's the *magister ludi*, in charge of organising everything. They say if the spectacles are a success, Titus will give him a villa at Baiae and a townhouse in Rome. But if not he could lose his head.'

Nubia saw Fabius approach a stocky man in a cream tunic who had appeared with the gladiators. Beside her, Bar pointed. 'I think that's Rotundus, the lanista.'

'What is lanista?' asked Nubia.

'A lanista is a trainer and manager,' said Bar. 'I don't suppose you can read?'

'Yes, I am learning.'

'Can you read the banner those two men are holding?'

'It is saying ... Ludus Aureus.'

'Then that is Rotundus. The Ludus Aureus is the new gladiator school here in Rome and he's the lanista. Hey! See that gladiator with the curly blond hair?'

Nubia nodded.

'That's Crescens. He's one of the most famous of the retiarii.'

'What is retee aree?'

'Net-men. They fight with a net, trident and dagger. And I think that one down there is Celadus the Thracian. There. The bald one.'

'My brother is a gladiator,' said Nubia.

Bar stared at her. 'Your brother is a gladiator?'

She nodded. 'He was taken as slave and is training to be a gladiator in the school of Capua. He is very far from Rome.'

'Capua!' breathed the young Syrian. 'It's the best school in Italia. Father and I were there last year. That's where Spartacus came from.'

'Spartacus?' The name sounded familiar to Nubia.

'Yes,' whispered Bar, though they were quite alone.

'He was a gladiator who lived a hundred and fifty years ago. But his legend lives on. He escaped from the school of Capua and he was so well-trained that he and some other runaway slaves survived for two years before they were recaptured.'

'Maybe my brother will escape, too,' whispered Nubia.

'I hope he doesn't try,' said Bar, giving her a quick glance, 'or he'll suffer the same fate as Spartacus.'

'What was that?'

'Spartacus and his six thousand runaway slaves were crucified,' said Bar in a low voice. 'Capua may be far away, but the whole road from here to there was lined with their crosses.'

'Juno!' squealed Flavia, as a finger tapped her shoulder.

And then, 'Oh Lupus! It's you. You frightened me halfway to Tartarus!' She pressed a hand to her thumping heart. Tigris had greeted Lupus with a brief wag, and was now sniffing the boy's sandals with great interest.

'Here,' hissed Flavia, tugging the sleeve of Lupus's tunic. 'Come here behind this column. I think this is the Emperor's box. Did you find Jonathan?'

Lupus shook his head and started to write on his wax tablet:

LOTS OF JEWS

'Who?' said Flavia. 'Where?' Then her eyes widened. 'You mean the criminals to be executed are Jews?'

Lupus nodded.

'But Jonathan wasn't with them?'

Lupus shook his head.

Flavia leaned her forehead on one of the cold, smooth columns. Beside her Tigris whined and turned in a circle.

'I'm sorry, Tigris,' she whispered.

Jonathan's big puppy moved to the marble balustrade. He stood on his hind legs to put his front paws on the marble half wall.

Lupus joined him, standing beside a big polished column and gazing out over the arena. He grunted in amazement and turned to beckon Flavia.

She joined him and Tigris at the parapet. And gasped.

Hundreds of gladiators and their attendants had filled the arena, and now they stood quietly, attentively, watching Fabius. He snapped a command Flavia could not hear, and the five hundred men turned to face Flavia and Lupus.

Flavia jerked back behind the shelter of her column and pressed her back to its cold curved surface. Then she peeked again.

Between her and Lupus, Jonathan's big puppy was still

standing at the low marble parapet, his eyes half closed and his nose testing the air.

As one, the gladiators stretched out their right hands towards Tigris.

'Hail, Caesar!' they cried. 'We salute you!'

Tigris wagged his tail at them.

And then – for the first time in a month – he began to bark.

SCROLL X

Lupus grabbed Tigris's lead and tugged, jerking the big puppy away from the balustrade.

'Oh, Pollux!' cursed Flavia. 'The guards have seen us!'

Lupus dragged Tigris down the polished marble stairs. As he ran down a narrow corridor he heard the slap of Flavia's sandalled feet close behind him. Lupus led her in the direction of a pearly orange light and a moment later they charged out from one of the big arched exits into the overcast March sunset.

Lupus could still hear the stamp of heavy hobnailed boots behind them.

'There!' cried Flavia. 'We can run behind those sand carts.'

He grunted and veered towards a line of carts waiting to unload.

'Hey, you kids! What were you doing in there? Stop!'

A soldier loomed up before him.

Lupus went left and Tigris went right, so that the puppy's lead was stretched taut. The soldier stumbled over it and pitched forward, coming down hard with a grunt and a clatter of metal armour.

'By the – come back, you pests!' he roared, struggling to his feet.

But Lupus was sprinting after Tigris, in the direction of the Forum. Flavia was ahead of him now, making for the carts up ahead.

They reached the carts and wove between one and the other until they reached the wet black marble cone. Lupus finally caught Tigris's lead, wrapped it round his wrist, and crouched down behind the fountain. Then he grunted a curse. Tigris had started to bark again.

'Shhh, Tigris!' gasped Flavia. 'We don't want the guards to find us. Shhh! Why's he barking now?' she asked Lupus. She put her hand gently round the puppy's muzzle, so that Tigris's barks became a whine.

Lupus shrugged. He was panting hard, too, and his heart was pounding, but he felt a grin spread across his face. He loved a good chase, especially when he escaped his pursuers.

Then his grin faded as he heard the slap of running feet on the other side of the fountain.

They had been discovered.

'Oh, Nubia, it's you!' cried Flavia. 'We thought it was the guard ... What a relief!'

Nubia nodded solemnly, and stared down at them. 'I heard Tigris,' she said. 'I was seeing the gladiators all look at Tigris in the amphitheatre and how he begins to bark. Then you run away so I come out of amphitheatre and see you running fast behind this big wet thing.'

'Just as well,' said Flavia, standing up and looking around. 'The sun is setting. It will be dark in less than an hour. I think the three of us had better get back.'

'Where is the Caudex?' said Nubia. 'We cannot return without him.'

'Nubia, you're right! He was supposed to meet us here. Where can he be?'

'Sisyphus!' cried Flavia, rushing into Senator Cornix's study. 'Where is everybody?'

'Finishing their dinner.' He stood with his back to them, unrolling a papyrus scroll. 'But I'm not speaking to you.'

'Why not?'

'You went investigating without me. I'm sulking.' He glanced over his shoulder and Flavia sighed with relief. His dark eyes were sparkling.

'Oh Sisyphus, I'm sorry! We were going to invite you but you weren't here. And so we went with Caudex and Aulus to – are they back?'

'Young Aulus is here, but I haven't seen Caudex ...' He put the scroll back in its case and turned to them. 'Now come along to the kitchen and I'll see if Niobe can spare three bowls of soup,' he said. 'Then you can tell me what you discovered.'

Early the next morning – before dawn – Nubia and her friends joined the senator and his family in the torchlit atrium for the first day of the inaugural games.

Senator Cornix stood before the household shrine, his head covered by a fold of his toga. When he had invoked the protection of the family genius and household gods he uncovered his head and waited for each of his children to greet him.

'Good morning, pater,' they all said as they filed past him in the flickering torchlight, and each gave him a respectful nod. All except for Rhoda, who ran to her father and hugged his knees.

The senator firmly detached her, but there was a twinkle in his eye and he kissed the top of her head.

'Good morning, Uncle Aulus,' Flavia said politely. 'Thank you again for letting us stay and for taking us to the games today. Is Caudex back?'

He frowned and shook his head. 'We will make an offering and a prayer for his safe return. Good morning, Nubia.'

'Good morning Uncle Aulus,' said Nubia. The smell of smoke from the torches always made her think of adventure. At home in Ostia they only got up before dawn when there was a mystery to solve.

The senator smiled with his eyes. 'And good morning to you, Lupus.'

The mute boy nodded respectfully.

Like the rest of them, Lupus was wearing a white tunic for the games. Nubia thought it made him look quite noble. He could easily be mistaken for one of the senator's own children.

But there was sadness in Lupus's face.

Tigris was sad, too. Jonathan's big puppy lay beside the impluvium with his chin on his paws, watching the torchlit activity around him with solemn eyes.

As the others collected their cloaks and napkins from pegs in the shadowy vestibule, Nubia knelt and patted him.

'I'm sorry Tigris,' she whispered. 'I know you like the gladiators but no dogs are allowed. You wait here and if Caudex comes back, tell him where we are.'

Before Flavia, a bright lopsided moon hung in a vibrant, deep blue sky. Behind her the sun had not yet risen. But she saw that in spite of the early hour, the area outside the amphitheatre was packed with thousands of excited people.

'Here we are,' said Senator Cornix presently, looking from his ivory ticket up at the numerals above the arch. 'Entrance number seventy.' He led them through the arch and up stairs to the first level. 'My dear,' he gently guided his wife and children away from the flow of excited, chattering Romans, 'let's meet back here at the midday break. Over there by the statue of Orpheus.'

'Whatever you say,' said Cynthia with a sigh.

Flavia frowned. 'Aren't we going with you?'

Aulus turned and smirked at her. 'Pater and I are going to sit in the senators' seats on this level,' he said. 'But women, slaves and *children* have to go up to the attic. Way, way up there. Too bad, isn't it? You really won't be able to see much at all.'

Flavia stuck out her tongue at his retreating back and then turned with a sigh to follow the others.

A chill breeze that often accompanied the sunrise touched in the highest level of the amphitheatre, and Nubia pulled her lionskin cloak tighter round her shoulders. She settled herself on the cushion Lady Cynthia's slave-girl had placed on the wooden seat. She looked up above her. The stars in the dawn sky had all faded and the blue was growing brighter by the moment. She looked down at the arena below her.

And her stomach did a flip.

From this lofty seat, the arena was tiny. So small that she could blot it out with both hands extended at arm's length.

Flavia voiced Nubia's thoughts. 'Aunt Cynthia! From

up here we won't be able to see anything! Why do we have to sit so high?'

Her aunt looked at her and sighed. 'I know. It's ridiculous. We might as well be watching ants scurrying about on an anthill. But it's considered decadent for proper Roman matrons and highborn children to watch people impersonating other people. We should count ourselves lucky we're here at all.'

'Frankly, I'm relieved,' said Sisyphus, who had elected to come with them. 'I can't stand the sight of blood. It makes me nauseous! And at least we're in the front row of this section, and none of those columns are blocking our view. Plus,' he gestured at the wooden roof above them, 'we'll be in the shade. It's chilly now but just wait until noon!'

Nubia looked around. The wooden seats around and behind her were filling up quickly, mostly with chattering women and children. The only men up here were slaves.

She turned to Sisyphus. 'Why are there only women and childs up here? And slaves?'

He arched one dark eyebrow. 'My dear girl, the merest glance at the seats below you will teach you more about the Roman class system than seventy scrolls and ten tutors. See those coloured marble columns and pediment? Looks like a little temple? No, way down there. Right by the arena. The columns with garlands draped between them.'

'Yes,' said Nubia.

'Well, that's the Imperial Box, where the Emperor will sit. The more important you are in Roman society, the closer you are to that box. All the other seats on that level are for senators. Except for the box which is opposite the Emperor's. That's for the Vestal Virgins. We can't see them from here, their box is covered, like the Emperor's.'

Nubia nodded solemnly and he pointed.

'Equestrians and government officials sit on that level, too, but behind the senators. Then, on the next tier up you have the well-to-do plebs: merchants, soldiers, successful freedmen and wealthy foreigners. Finally, on the third level – the one just below us – are the poorest people and slaves. They are the lowest in the pecking order.'

'Why are we very higher than poor slaves?' asked Nubia. 'Are we below the lowest pecking?'

'It's not that,' said Sisyphus. 'A senator's wife – for example – is worth far more than a male slave. No, the reason women and children are way up here is so they won't be corrupted by the violence and blood.'

Nubia nodded and glanced at the twins, who had decided to sit either side of her. They both wore identical tin gladiator helmets with coloured pigeon feathers, red for Quintus and yellow for Sextus. On Nubia's right – on the other side of Quintus – sat Lupus, Flavia and Sisyphus. Then came Lady Cynthia with Rhoda on her lap. To Nubia's left – on the other side of Sextus – sat Hyacinth and a slave-girl called Prisca.

Quintus was stroking Nubia's lionskin cloak. He gazed up at her with huge eyes from under the brim of his tin helmet. 'Did you kill this lion?' he lisped.

Nubia shook her head. 'No. This cloak is gift. It is thanks for when I was conquering a lion. But he is most tame lion called Monobaz.'

'Monobaz?' cried Sisyphus. 'He's mentioned on the programme.'

'Oh, let me see!' cried Flavia, snatching the sheet of papyrus from Sisyphus. He gave a mock sigh and winked at Nubia.

Flavia held out the programme at arm's length in order that they could all see. Nubia tried to follow as Flavia read in her clear voice:

PROGRAMME OF EVENTS

INAUGURAL GAMES DAY I
TO BE HELD AT THE NEW AMPHITHEATRE

OPENING PROCESSION

TIGHTROPE WALKERS

BEAST COMBAT

featuring Monobaz v Saevus

A HUNT OF EXOTIC BEASTS

including camelopard, lions and unicorn

PARADE OF INFORMERS

EXECUTION OF CRIMINALS

a parricide will die re-enacting the abduction of Ganymede
a thief will die re-enacting the death of Laureolus
Jewish zealots will fight bears with curved daggers

COMBAT OF NOVELTY GLADIATOR PAIRS

featuring women
COMBAT OF GLADIATORS

AWNINGS AND DRINKS WILL BE PROVIDED
PRIZES WILL BE DISTRIBUTED

Nubia looked at Sisyphus. 'Women are fighting as gladiators?'

He nodded. 'That's another reason the women are way up here,' he whispered. 'The senators are afraid their wives might get ideas!'

Nubia gazed at Sisyphus.

'It's a novelty act to whet the appetite. To amuse the crowds before the real competitions start. Sometimes they have pygmies or cripples fight each other.'

Nubia shuddered and looked around. It was only an hour past dawn but already the amphitheatre was nearly full. Wherever she looked she saw people.

On their level but across the vast space in between, she caught sight of a dark-skinned family. They looked Nubian. It was a mother with her three children and two fair-skinned slave-girls attending them. Nubia swallowed and blinked back the tears blurring her vision. She would never sit laughing with her mother and brothers again.

Then she felt a small hot hand slip into hers. It was five-year-old Quintus, on her right. He had been watching her. At the same moment she felt Sextus grip her left hand and – as if they had rehearsed it – they both leant their tin-helmeted heads against her shoulders.

This made Nubia want to cry even more and she felt the familiar tightness in her throat. But a blare of trumpets made her forget her sadness. The games had begun.

SCROLL XI

'Look!' Flavia pointed down into the arena. 'Titus is marching in the procession!'

Sisyphus nodded. 'I wonder where his brother is. There's a rumour Domitian is sulking because Titus is getting so much glory.'

'How do you know so much?' whispered Flavia.

'I keep my eyes and ears open.' Sisyphus leaned forward in his seat. 'But I don't know everything. For example, I don't know which one of those men down there is the notorious Fabius.'

Flavia pointed down into the arena. 'There. The man with the ponytail in the white tunic, walking behind the trumpet players.'

'Ah!' said Sisyphus, his dark eyes fixed on the distant figure.

'Why is he notorious?' asked Flavia.

Sisyphus pressed his lips together.

'Why?' she persisted. Lupus, Nubia and Hyacinth leaned in, too.

'My dears, I don't know if I dare tell!'

'Oh please, Sisyphus!'

'Very well.' Sisyphus lowered his voice to a dramatic whisper. 'They say Fabius used to be a Stoic, like poor old Seneca. He always objected to the spectacles on moral grounds, because he thought bloodshed was barbaric.

Then one day his friends forced him to come along with them. He went, but he refused to watch. He kept his eyes closed right through the acrobats and the animal fights. Then – during the beast hunt – the crowd gave such a resounding yell that he opened his eyes to see why they were shouting.'

'What happened?' asked Flavia.

'The moment Fabius opened his eyes and saw the blood, he fell in love with it!' said Sisyphus, keeping his voice as low as the crowd's cheering would allow.

Lupus gave Sisyphus his bug-eyed look and Nubia said, 'He fell in love with blood?'

Sisyphus nodded and widened his kohl-rimmed eyes. 'Bloodlust. It happens to some people,' he said. 'Now Fabius can't get enough blood. He longs for the beast fights when tigers and lions fight with dripping teeth. He craves the violent death of criminals, ripped apart by wild animals. And most of all he loves the gladiator fights. He always puts his thumb down because he wants to see blood.'

Flavia realised her mouth was hanging open. She closed it and glanced round. Her aunt was arranging Rhoda's hair, which had come unpinned, but Lupus, Nubia, Hyacinth and even the twins were all watching Sisyphus wide-eyed.

Sisyphus nodded sadly. 'That was why Fabius became an organiser. Because of his bloodlust. Once he was watching a particularly violent combat between gladiators. The secutor cut off the net-man's head and the blood pumped out like a fountain, making a big red pool as the headless man sank slowly to the sand.'

'Ewww,' said Flavia

'Tac!' Sisyphus put up a hand to still her. 'They say that Fabius was so overcome by the sight of all that blood that he rushed forward, knelt on the sand and lapped it up like a dog!'

'EWWW!' everyone cried.

Nubia looked at Sisyphus. 'Why are they doing this? Why are Romans always making the blood to flow?'

'Blood pleases the dead,' said Sisyphus. 'Games like these were first given at funerals, to appease the dead person.'

Nubia frowned. 'But why blood?'

'It's always blood,' said Flavia.

Sisyphus nodded. 'Blood is power.'

'Blood is life.' Aunt Cynthia's voice from the end of the bench was husky.

They all looked at her, but she kept her eyes on the arena.

'I suppose that's true,' said Flavia after a moment's thought. 'Admiral Pliny says the cure for epilepsy is to drink a cup of warm gladiator's blood. Some barbarians drink horses' blood. And Christians drink the blood of their god. Jonathan told me that.'

IT'S REALLY WINE wrote Lupus.

Sisyphus nodded. 'Some people believe the strength – the essence of a person – lies in their blood. Drink the blood, get the power.'

Lupus wrote on his wax tablet:

HOW DO YOU GET BLOODLUST?

'It comes in through your eyes,' said Sisyphus, lowering his voice. 'And it often possesses the gentlest, the kindest, the most refined people ...' He darted a look at Lady Cynthia, who had bent her head over Rhoda again.

Flavia glanced at her aunt and raised her eyebrows at Sisyphus.

He gave a tiny nod, almost imperceptible, then leaned over to whisper in Flavia's ear. 'That's the real reason the Senator is leaving town tomorrow.'

The sun was well up when the tightrope walkers concluded their display with an act that brought fifty thousand Romans gasping to their feet.

It was a tightrope-walking elephant.

Nubia found herself standing, too.

'Behold ... look!' she cried. 'The elephant walks on rope!'

'Melephant!' squealed Rhoda, jumping up and down on the bench beside her mother.

'He's wonderful,' said Hyacinth.

'Melephant!' laughed the twins, and then chanted: 'Melephant, melephant!' along with Rhoda.

Flavia laughed. 'He is amazing!' she agreed. 'Look how hard he's concentrating.'

Nubia felt an intense compassion for the ponderous creature, making his way delicately across the arena on a rope which from this distance seemed little more than a thread. The amphitheatre was utterly silent and now even the twins were still. Nubia kept her eyes on the elephant, afraid that if she took her eyes away, he might fall.

But he did not fall and as he stepped onto the safety of a ramp the vast space of the amphitheatre erupted in cheers.

With barely a pause, the water organ played a dramatic chord, the trumpets blared and the crowd chattered excitedly as two creatures whirled onto the sand of the arena below them.

'One of them is a bear, but what's the animal with the horn? Nubia?'

'I am not knowing his name in Latin.'

'Rhinoceros,' said Sisyphus. 'We use the Greek word.'

'Why are they being chained together?' asked Nubia.

'It forces them to fight each other,' said Sisyphus. And he shuddered.

'Look, Mama!' chorused the twins. 'Bear!'

'That's not just any bear,' said Sisyphus. 'That is a Nubian bear. They are the fiercest bear in the world. Correct, Nubia?'

But Nubia had covered her eyes.

Nubia did not watch the rhino gore the bear with his horn and then trample him into a pulp. Nor, in the next beast combat, did she see the leopard bring down a terrified giraffe and feed on its still-living body.

She couldn't bear to watch the elephant fight the bull, and even when Flavia described how the victorious elephant lifted the huge dead creature on its tusks she refused to look.

But when Lupus hopped up and down on his seat and Flavia squealed 'Monobaz!' then Nubia uncovered her eyes.

A beautiful golden lion with a dark mane had entered the arena

Nubia gripped Flavia's arm.

'It is!' she cried. 'Alas! It is the Monobaz! And they are going to make him fight a beast!'

Flavia was studying the programme. 'Saevus,' she said, 'He's going to fight Saevus.'

Nubia's heart stuttered and she gazed at Flavia in horror. 'But doesn't that word mean …' Her voice trailed off, and Flavia nodded grimly.

'Saevus means "savage"!'

SCROLL XII

Lupus laughed as Monobaz's opponent hopped into the amphitheatre. It seemed minuscule from this distance.

'What is it?' asked Flavia. 'It's just a dot from up here ...'

'It is little black rabbit,' said Nubia, and a smile spread across her lovely face.

The catcalls and laughs were stilled by a thundering roar from Monobaz, who had crouched on the sand. The rabbit fearlessly hopped forward.

Now the crowd was utterly silent as the dark rabbit and golden lion approached one another. Suddenly the rabbit charged. Monobaz turned and loped away from the rabbit and the crowd laughed and clapped in delight. The water organ played a jaunty tune. For several minutes the bunny chased the black-maned lion around the sandy oval.

Lupus saw that many of those in the crowd were pointing at the Imperial Box. The Emperor had risen to his feet and had folded his arms across his purple chest. Even from this distance Lupus could make out a scowl on Titus's face as he turned to say something to a bald man in a toga, who stood behind him. Lupus saw the man shake his head and point down at the arena floor. Lupus looked too and saw that finally the lion had stopped to face his foe.

Saevus the rabbit charged one last time.

Straight into Monobaz's open mouth.

'Oh!' cried Flavia, Nubia, Hyacinth and a thousand other soft-hearted Romans. A sympathetic chord from the water organ echoed the crowd's lament and then died away.

Monobaz stood, padded over towards the Imperial Box, and looked up. Then he opened his great mouth and the arena erupted with cheers and laughter as the rabbit hopped down, apparently unharmed.

Titus applauded and laughed. Then he gave the two animals a thumbs-up to show he approved.

To thunderous applause – and triumphant chords from the water organ – the hopping bunny led Monobaz out of the arena.

Nubia turned to Lupus and Flavia. 'I like the games,' she said with a smile. 'They are not so bad as I feared!'

But even as she spoke the trumpets blared again and a hundred wild beasts poured into the arena from a dozen side entrances. There were bears, lions, wild boar, leopards and one creature with a single horn in the middle of its forehead. The crowd gasped.

'Look, Nubia!' cried Flavia. 'A unicorn!'

'Look!' echoed the twins. 'A unicorn! A unicorn!'

'Municorn!' squealed Rhoda.

'No,' whispered Nubia. 'It is just an antelope. They make two horns one when he is young...'

'He's beautiful!' said Hyacinth. 'How do they make his two horns one, Nubia?'

'Yes, tell us!' laughed Flavia.

'When the horns are still soft they twist them together. It hurts them because –'

But Nubia could not finish. Her hand went automatically to her throat. Even from this distance she caught a whiff of scent rising from the animals on the sand below.

It was the smell of fear.

Flavia managed to watch for a while. At first the animals had not wanted to fight. They hugged the inner net in silent fear. But slaves prodded them with red-hot rods and finally the creatures began to attack one another.

It helped that they were far enough away to look like toys.

Presently one of the lions buried his face in the unicorn's belly and Flavia had to turn away. Even from this height she could see the lion's beautiful prey was still alive.

As she turned her head, she saw her aunt leaning forward with parted lips and bright eyes. Little Rhoda was looking wide-eyed from her mother to the animals and back. She was not crying but she was tugging her mother's stola.

Flavia could not hear Rhoda over the roaring crowd, but she could see her lips moving. Cynthia was oblivious.

The little girl's lower lip began to quiver so Flavia beckoned her over. Rhoda came to Flavia and climbed onto her lap.

'Lion is eating municorn,' she said in Flavia's ear.

Flavia nodded sadly. 'I know.'

Rhoda put her thumb in her mouth and turned her head to watch. Flavia kept her own face averted.

Presently the water organ played a chord loud enough to be heard above the crowd. Flavia forced herself to look back down just in time to see the hunters run barefoot into the arena.

Lupus nodded with approval as the hunters came on. Their timing was perfect. The predators had settled down to feed on their victims and the beast fight threatened to become boring.

There were six hunters. Three men and three women. They wore white tunics and padded white leggings, but no shoes. The women held bows and the men had hunting spears. None of them had any protective armour.

Behind him he heard a woman's hysterical cry. 'Carpophorus! Carpophorus!'

And then a shrill cry from right beside them: 'Carpo!' It was Flavia's aunt Cynthia. Lupus followed her gaze.

Carpophorus must be the fair-skinned youth with a mane of tawny hair. It was hard to tell from this distance and this angle, but he seemed a head taller than the others.

The crowd gasped as he charged the lion who had killed the unicorn. The lion raised his face from the creature's belly and the entire amphitheatre erupted in a resounding cheer as Carpophorus plunged his spear deep into the lion's chest. As usual, the water organ punctuated this thrust with a deep, dramatic chord.

'Isn't he magnificent?' shouted Sisyphus above the cheers. 'He's only seventeen years old, but already he's known throughout the Empire.'

For a long minute the youth and lion struggled over the carcass of the unicorn. Even from this distance Lupus could see the hunter's muscles bulge as he held the raging lion at bay. One false move might alter the balance. The spear could break like a toothpick and the lion would take the hunter in his bloody jaws. The chords of the water organ climbed higher and higher as the tension built.

Lupus watched in admiration as the tawny youth continued to hold the lion at bay, waiting until all its blood had pumped out onto the unicorn. Presently the lion slumped onto the body of its victim and Carpophorus wrenched the spear free.

The water organ sang. The crowd cheered.

Carpo did not even pause to acknowledge his triumph. He turned immediately to attack the bear, which had seized one of the female beast-fighters and was embracing the woman in a terrifying hug.

In a magnificent two-handed arc, Carpophorus drove his spear into the bear's back. The Roman ladies around Lupus went wild, and it seemed the whole amphitheatre was chanting: 'Car-PO! Car-PO!'

The bear opened his mouth in a roar which could not be heard, dropped the girl, and began to pursue Carpophorus.

Carpophorus danced backwards before the bear, who was staggering forward on its hind legs like a man, the spear still protruding from its back. It batted at the young beast-fighter, first with one paw, then with the other. The crowd was voicing its support and Lupus realised he, too, was screaming with his tongueless mouth.

But then Carpophorus let the bear come too close. The crowd gasped and the water organ groaned.

'The bear got him,' screamed a matron a few rows behind. 'The bear got Carpo!'

Sure enough, Lupus saw a dark stain begin to bloom

on the white tunic stretched across the beast-fighter's chest.

Suddenly Sisyphus yelped. Lady Cynthia had swooned onto his lap.

SCROLL XIII

By the time Sisyphus managed to revive Lady Cynthia and Lupus turned his attention back to the show, Carpophorus had vanquished the bear and was pursuing a huge boar. A quick glance showed Lupus that most of the other beast-fighters were either dead or wounded. One of them – a dark-skinned woman – had lost her bow and was wrestling a leopard barehanded. Lupus alternated his concentration between Carpophorus and the venatrix.

Carpophorus was apparently unaware of the gash across his chest, even though the front of his tunic was now dark with blood. He had speared the boar and was struggling to keep it at bay. The bristling creature had squirmed halfway up his spear and its wickedly curved tusks were almost within range of the hero's padded thigh.

Suddenly the crowd gasped. For no apparent reason the leopard had writhed away from the dark-skinned venatrix and was approaching Carpophorus from behind.

The leopard crouched, tail twitching. The crowd and the water organ sang out a warning.

As the leopard launched itself into the air Carpophorus jumped aside.

Resounding cheers as the leopard landed on the wounded boar and Carpophorus rolled safely on the sand. He was on his feet in a moment, and, grasping a fallen comrade's spear, he returned to the fighting animals. He raised his arms high above his head.

A momentary pause.

Then he plunged the spear downwards, impaling both leopard and boar in one powerful stroke and pinning them to the arena floor. As a massive cheer resounded around the amphitheatre, Carpo turned towards the people and lifted his hands in a gesture of victory.

The crowd went wild.

As Flavia watched the blood-soaked, tawny-haired hunter help the female beast-fighter to her feet she realised that she was on her feet. When had she stood up? Everyone around her was standing, too, but now some were beginning to sit down again. Gratefully, Flavia lowered her weight to the cushioned bench and watched the two distant beast-fighters pick their way among the carcasses of animals and the corpses of men to stand before the Emperor's box.

They knelt on the sandy floor of the arena, and Titus tossed something to each of them.

'Bags of gold,' said Sisyphus, shouting to make himself heard above the roar of the crowd.

Flavia's knees were trembling violently now that she had taken her weight off them, and so she put her hands on them to stop them. But her knees were still moving so much that she laughed at the strangeness of it. She suddenly felt intensely alive and full of an inexplicable joy.

The two surviving beast-fighters were leaving the arena now and Flavia surrendered herself to the crowd's mood.

'Car-PO! Car-PO! Car-PO!' she cried along with thousands of others. And although she was shouting with all her might, she could not even hear her own voice above the roar.

It was late morning and warm enough for Flavia to shrug off her blue palla.

The dead animals had been dragged from the arena with hooks and fresh sand raked over the patches soaked by blood. Now the water organ was playing a slow, thumping tune that reminded Flavia of a funeral dirge.

'What is happening now?' asked Nubia. 'Who are all those marching?'

'Let me look.' Flavia consulted her papyrus pro-gramme. 'Oh. It's the Parade of Informers.'

'What is that?'

'I'm not sure.'

'Informers!' Sisyphus spat out a date stone. 'The lowest breed of creature on earth. They spy on other people and if they see someone doing the least thing wrong they take him to court. If they win their case they share out the poor fellow's estate with the Emperor.'

'There are so many of them,' said Nubia.

'And some of them are senators!' gasped Flavia. 'See the broad stripes on their tunics?'

Sisyphus nodded grimly. 'Titus can't execute highborn men here in the amphitheatre. But for men of rank – like those men – the shame of being paraded in front of their peers is almost worse than death.'

'Behold ... Look!' said Nubia. 'What is around their necks?'

Lupus made a V with his forearms and locked them around his neck.

'Yes, you're right, Lupus,' said Flavia. 'They're wearing

some kind of yoke which makes them look up.'

'Ha!' Sisyphus clapped his hands and looked at them bright-eyed. 'They're wearing wooden forks. That's where we get the word –'

'Furcifer!' squealed Flavia. 'Scoundrel! It means someone wearing a fork!'

Sisyphus nodded. 'The wooden forks force them to keep their heads up, so that people can see who they are.'

AND THROW THINGS AT THEM

wrote Lupus, as members of the jeering crowd began pelting the informers with eggs and rotten lettuces.

Sisyphus held out a papyrus twist full of dates. Lupus took a handful and hurled them towards the informers. They fell short, raining down on some senators in the lowest tier.

Lupus hurriedly crouched below the low wooden wall and made his 'Oops' face back up at them.

Sisyphus gave him a look. 'They're for us, not the informers,' he said dryly, and extended the papyrus cone towards Flavia.

Flavia grasped a handful but Nubia shook her head without taking her eyes from the scene below her. Flavia suddenly remembered the first time she had seen Nubia being led to the slave market, naked and chained at the neck.

'What sorts of things do informers report?' Flavia asked Sisyphus quickly, hoping to distract Nubia.

'Oh, real or imagined plots against the Emperor, criticism of his rule ... anything,' Sisyphus popped a date in his mouth. 'In Nero's time they bred like maggots in rotten meat. Good for Titus, I say, exposing them for who they are.'

'What will they do to them afterwards?' asked Flavia. 'Are they going to kill them?'

'No,' said Sisyphus. 'The lowborn ones might be auctioned off as slaves and those of senatorial class will be deported to some barren island.'

'Ah,' said Flavia, nodding wisely and removing a date stone from her mouth. 'Exile.'

'What is exile?' asked Nubia.

'It's when you are sent far away from your home, with no hope of ever returning,' said Flavia, then bit her lip as she saw the expression on Nubia's face.

Sisyphus waved the papyrus programme sheet and said: 'The next event is an execution. That man killed his father.'

Nubia saw two guards prodding a man around the arena. Behind them walked a slave with a sign on a stick. Even from this distance Nubia could make out the criminal's long curly yellow hair and red lips. Apart from a tiny loincloth, he was naked. Curses and catcalls erupted from the crowds and some of those on the lower levels tossed the last of their rotten fruit at him.

Flavia leaned forward and squinted at the sign carried by the slave. 'I plunged a sword in my father's throat,' she read.

'Murderer!' screeched a harsh female voice behind Nubia.

Nubia turned to glance at the people in the row behind her. The young matron was pretty, but hatred contorted her face and made it ugly. Then – even as Nubia watched – the hatred was replaced by delighted surprise.

Nubia turned and gasped.

A winged man was flying straight at her.

SCROLL XIV

Nubia cringed as the man flew towards her. So did the others in the surrounding seats. All except for Lupus, who uttered a bark of laughter.

Then Nubia realised what it was: a man with feathered wings attached to his arms.

His tunic was covered in feathers, too, and he wore yellow leggings to make his legs look like an eagle's. The man's skin was dark brown like hers, and the feathers matched perfectly. He flapped his wings comically, but above the imitation beak his eyes showed fierce concentration. The birdman swung past her, so close that she felt a breeze on her face. The next instant he was spiralling down towards the arena below. People in the other sections of the arena shrank back and shrieked with delight.

Nubia saw thousands of faces looking up in wonder, laughing, exclaiming, pointing. Many – like Lupus – were trying to see what was holding the birdman up. The man-eagle flew back again, this time towards those on the lower level, and now Nubia could see the thin ropes that held him.

She followed the line of the cords up to see the dark silhouettes against the blue sky. There were men at the top of the amphitheatre standing on the ropes which held the coloured sheets of cloth. They were operating a complicated system of ropes and pulleys.

Down on the sandy floor of the arena the convicted criminal looked as small as a desert mouse. He had heard the crowd gasping and he was looking around in terror for the beast that was to devour him. It had not yet occurred to him to look up.

Nubia heard the women around her taunting him.

'You're in for it now, Ganymede!'

'Here's Jupiter!'

'Bye-bye, parricide!'

Flavia turned bright-eyed to Nubia. 'It's from a myth. Jupiter liked a beautiful boy called Ganymede and took the form of an eagle to kidnap him. He carried him off to Mount Olympus and Ganymede served wine to the gods and goddesses ... according to the legend.'

The water organ had been sounding ominous chords but now, as 'Ganymede' finally spotted the descending birdman and ran, it began to play a comical tune. All around Nubia people were laughing, even Flavia, Lupus and the twins.

'Watch out, Ganymede!' screamed the woman in the row behind them. 'Jupiter likes you!'

'Better run away!' shouted a boy from somewhere to their left.

Little Rhoda laughed, too. 'Big bird chases man!'

'Oh!' gasped thousands of people as the birdman almost grasped his prey.

Ganymede had writhed from Jupiter's grasp this time, but Nubia knew he couldn't hold out forever. Presently he stumbled and fell and the bird grasped the long-haired criminal round the waist. Suddenly they were rising fast, not spiralling but moving straight up.

The nearly-naked criminal was struggling in his

captor's arms when something detached itself and fell to the sand below. His curly yellow hair.

'Hey, Ganymede!' screamed the woman behind them. 'You dropped your wig!'

The terrified man had stopped squirming. Nubia saw Lupus nod grimly and exchange a knowing glance with Sisyphus. She guessed what they were thinking: if the man fell from the eagle's grip at this height, the fall would shatter him.

The water organ was playing a dramatic series of chords that mounted higher and higher up the scale as the two men rose up through the vast space. Presently they were at her level. Lupus looked up in order to see the men working the cords, but Nubia couldn't take her eyes from Ganymede's terror-struck face.

When the birdman and his prey could go no higher, and were silhouettes against the fresh blue sky, the trumpets suddenly blared. This must have been the birdman's cue: he let go of Ganymede.

With a guttural shriek the criminal fell, his legs and arms pumping wildly, as if the empty space around him might suddenly grow solid. As he plummeted, Nubia's stomach seemed to plunge with him. Down and down he fell, and a great cheer rose up from the throng as he struck the arena far below with a puff of sand.

The sand settled over the crumpled body.

Suddenly Nubia cried out as the body twitched.

The criminal was still alive.

SCROLL XV

Nubia watched as a figure in dark robes and a white mask stepped into the arena and walked over to the broken man.

'I think that's supposed to be Pluto,' said Sisyphus.

'Pluto,' Flavia said to Nubia, 'is the god who rules the Underworld.'

'And he's about to claim poor Ganymede for his kingdom,' said Sisyphus.

The masked man lifted something like a mallet and for a moment he seemed to hesitate. Then he ended the broken man's life with a swift downward blow.

Nubia lowered her head between her knees and breathed deeply in short little gasps.

Lupus patted her back.

'Are you all right, Nubia?' Flavia leaned forward and whispered. 'It's easier if you imagine they're dolls and not real people.'

'Mummy,' came Rhoda's clear voice. 'Why did that man fall down?'

'He was a wicked man.' Cynthia's voice. 'He killed his daddy.'

'He killed daddy?'

'Not your daddy. His own daddy.'

'Why?'

'I don't know, dear.'

'Mummy, can I go to the latrine?'

Cynthia sighed. 'Yes, dear. I'll take you. Sisyphus, did you notice where the latrines are located?'

'I think they're two levels down, Lady Cynthia. Shall I accompany you?'

'No, thank you. We can manage.' Cynthia nodded to her slave-girl. 'Come, Prisca.'

Nubia's nausea was subsiding. She lifted her head and twisted on her wooden seat to let them pass. The twins were going, too, leaving their tin helmets atop their cushions on the wooden bench. It was nearly noon and pleasantly warm.

Sisyphus extended a water-gourd to Nubia. She took it, drank and handed it back.

Suddenly something about the scene seemed utterly familiar.

The excited babble of the people around her, the vast space before her, the pure light coming from above, Flavia drinking from the gourd, Lupus yawning ...

'What's the matter, Nubia?' asked Flavia, passing the gourd to Lupus.

Nubia shook her head, then said, 'I have dreamed this most exactly.'

'Oh, I have that sometimes,' said Flavia. 'You feel you've been here before?'

Lupus nodded, too.

'Yes,' said Nubia. 'I have been here before.'

'You know what that means, don't you?' Sisyphus raised his eyebrows at her.

'No.'

'It means you're exactly where the gods want you to be.'

'The gods want me to be in this place?'

'Yes. They sometimes give you dreams which you forget until you are in the place you dreamed. My old grandmother, may Juno preserve her soul, said that means you're on your life's path: in exactly the right place.'

'This is the right place?' Nubia stared at the crowds around her, then down at the distant sandy oval of the arena where slaves were raking fresh sand over dark patches.

'What's next?' murmured Flavia, picking up a sheet of papyrus from her aunt's seat. 'Oh! This isn't the programme. These are the highlights for the next few days ... Look at this, Nubia! Tomorrow they're going to kill five thousand animals. And it says – oh no!'

'What?' said Nubia.

'Lupus,' said Flavia. 'When you saw the prisoners who were condemned to death ... was Ganymede there, too?'

Lupus looked blankly at her.

'The man who killed his father, the man they just executed ... was he with the other prisoners?'

Lupus slowly shook his head and wrote on his wax tablet:

THEY WERE ALL JEWS

'That means there must be other prisoners being kept somewhere.'

Lupus frowned.

Flavia pointed to the programme. 'This sheet has highlights for the next few days,' she said. 'Look at who they're executing the day after tomorrow!'

EXECUTION OF CRIMINALS

DAY I

A PARRICIDE WILL DIE RE-ENACTING
THE ABDUCTION OF GANYMEDE

A THIEF WILL DIE RE-ENACTING
THE DEATH OF LAUREOLUS

JEWISH ZEALOTS WILL FIGHT BEARS
WITH CURVED DAGGERS

EVENING EVENT: A TRAITOR WILL DIE
THE DEATH OF LEANDER

DAY II

A MURDERER WILL DIE RE-ENACTING
THE STORY OF ORPHEUS

DAY III

AN ARSONIST WILL SUFFER
THE TORMENT OF PROMETHEUS

DAY IV

DAEDALUS WILL BE PUT INTO HIS MAZE WITH A BEAR

DAY V

A MURDERESS WILL RE-ENACT
THE SHAME OF PASIPHAE

DAY VI

A PLUNDERER OF TEMPLES WILL DIE
THE DEATH OF HERCULES

DAY VII

A RUNAWAY SLAVE WILL RE-ENACT
THE DEATH OF ACTAEON

Lupus pointed to the entry for day three and raised his eyebrows.

'That's the one,' said Flavia grimly. 'If Jonathan is alive, and if they think he started the fire, then he must be here somewhere. You just didn't find him. And the day after tomorrow they're going to kill him in the same way Prometheus was tortured.'

Nubia felt sick again. 'Alas!' she whispered. 'Prometheus was having his liver pecked out by a bird.'

'Mama, why is that man being tied to sticks?' Rhoda's voice piped brightly above the deep chords of the water organ.

'He's another bad man, dear,' said Flavia's aunt. 'He robbed people. They're crucifying him. Or perhaps a fierce beast is going to devour him. Let's see.'

'Laureolus,' said Flavia with a frown, studying the programme. 'I thought I knew all the myths but I don't remember a mythological character called Laureolus.'

'That's because he was a real person. I saw a play about him once ...' Sisyphus leaned over to look at the sheet in her hand.

'How did he die?' asked Flavia.

'His victims tied him to a cross and let a boar gore him.'

'Oh,' said Flavia, and then turned to Nubia. 'I don't think we want to watch this.'

'He's stopped screaming,' said Flavia presently. 'Does that mean I can look yet?'

'Don't ask me,' said Sisyphus in a muffled voice. 'I stopped watching when his leg came off.'

'The blood,' whispered Nubia. 'Look at all the blood.'

'Don't look,' said Flavia, and turned her head to see what Lupus was writing on his wax tablet.

HE'S STILL ALIVE

'But it's been nearly half an hour,' muttered Flavia. 'Or it feels like it.'

'I think I am going to be sick,' whispered Nubia.

'Me, too,' said Flavia. 'Let's go and find the latrines.'

Lupus sat forward on the bench as a blare of the trumpet and a herald announced the final event before the gladiatorial combats. The execution of one hundred Jewish zealots. It was fitting, proclaimed the herald, that these men should spill their blood, for they were some of the rebellious Jews who had caused Rome such trouble ten years ago.

As the water organ thumped out a sequence of sinister, discordant notes, Lupus watched the men stumble into the arena, shading their eyes against the pure spring sunshine. The crowd roared with anger, drowning out the music.

These were the prisoners he had seen the previous day; he recognised the rabbi. Almost immediately the bears moved into the arena. Unlike the animals which had come before them, these fearsome creatures did not need to be prodded with red-hot irons. They must have been trained to crave human flesh.

With breathtaking speed, one bear gripped a zealot in a deadly embrace. At this some of the Jews began to scream and run. Others – like the rabbi – stood and waited for death. A few fought back bravely with their little curved knives. Lupus saw that Sisyphus and Hyacinth had hidden their faces in their hands. The twins had grown bored with the distant executions and were playing toy gladiators on Nubia's seat cushion. Little Rhoda was fast asleep, thumb in mouth, on her mother's lap. But Lady Cynthia was oblivious. Her lips were parted and her clear grey eyes fixed on the scene of bloody carnage below.

Lupus could see she was drinking in every drop.

'Are you feeling better?' asked Flavia.

Nubia nodded and lifted her head from the fountain. Her knees were still trembling but her stomach felt more settled. The water, tinted pink with wine, had settled her stomach and cleared her mouth.

For the first time she noticed a marble statue in a niche behind the spouts: a man holding a lyre. The name carved in the base of the sculpture told who he was. Orpheus was so skilfully carved and painted that he looked like a real person. Someone had tied a white scarf over his eyes. Nubia looked around. All the other statues she could see were also blindfolded.

She pointed. 'Why?'

'Why the blindfolds?' said Flavia, wiping her mouth. 'So that the gods and heroes won't be upset by the sight of those wicked criminals. And all that blood.'

Nubia stared at her ex-mistress. These people let little children watch a man being slowly disembowelled but they covered up the eyes of their statues.

She would never understand the Romans. Never.

'Nuuuu!' Flavia uttered a strangled cry and Nubia whirled to see a hundred red balls raining down from the sky.

SCROLL XVI

Nubia lifted her hands to ward off the swarm of falling balls and as one smacked her right hand her fingers instinctively gripped it.

Around her people were screaming and diving. A few aisles below she saw three men struggling for something. Slowly Nubia opened her hand and gazed at the object lying in her palm. It was a red wooden ball, the size of a small apple.

'It's a lottery ball,' squealed Flavia, and clapped her hand over her own mouth. Then: 'Quickly! Hide it before someone sees it and murders you.'

Nubia stared at Flavia.

'Hide it now!'

Obediently, Nubia undid the string of her leather purse, pushed the ball into it and drew her lionskin cloak tightly around her.

'Come on!' hissed Flavia. 'Let's go back to our seats. Don't tell anyone you have it.'

'Why not?' Nubia felt Flavia's urgent hand on the small of her back, hurrying her up the stairs.

'It might be worth a fortune,' whispered Flavia.

'What do you mean?'

'Sisyphus was telling me earlier. The balls are hollow. There should be a piece of papyrus inside telling you what you've won.'

'I win something?'

'Yes! Sometimes they're just jokes. The papyrus might say you've won a basket of chickpeas. Or an ivory toothpick. But usually they're fabulous prizes. Like a horse, a slave, a ship, even a whole villa.'

'Oh,' said Nubia. 'I wonder what my ball is saying inside?'

'We'd better wait,' said Flavia, panting a little as they reached a landing on the marble stairs. 'It's too crowded here. You saw those men fighting for a ball, didn't you? Better not take it out until we get back to the house. Can you bear to wait till evening?'

But Nubia did not have to wait until that evening.

At their prearranged noon meeting, Senator Cornix took one look at his wife's unnaturally bright eyes and flushed cheeks and gruffly announced that they were going home immediately.

'But pater!' cried Aulus. 'The gladiators! We'll miss the gladiators. And there are female gladiators fighting this afternoon!'

'All the more reason to go,' the senator said between clenched teeth. 'And we're not leaving Rome tomorrow. We're leaving today!'

'I can't open it,' said Nubia. 'It is most sticky. Here Lupus. You try.'

She handed the red ball to Lupus who bent his head as he tried to unscrew the two hemispheres of the ball.

The three of them were in the girls' bedroom back at Senator Cornix's townhouse on the Caelian Hill. They had eaten lunch and now the sounds of a household packing drifted in through the open door.

'What are you doing?' asked Aulus, suddenly appearing over Nubia's shoulder.

'Nothing,' said Flavia, and Lupus quickly hid the ball under his cloak.

'You're hiding something. Show me!'

Slowly Lupus took out his wax tablet and opened it.

'See, Aulus?' Flavia forced herself to smile up at him. 'We were just making a plan of the amphitheatre, trying to remember where we sat today.'

'Well, Lupus hasn't drawn it right. It doesn't look like that. That's a stupid plan of the amphitheatre. The amphitheatre isn't oval. It's round.'

'No it's not,' said Flavia with a scowl. 'It's oval.'

'It's round.'

'Oval!'

'Round!'

'Aulus!' came the Senator's voice. 'Have you finished doing what I asked you to do?'

'Coming, Pater!' Aulus Junior shot Flavia a glare. 'Big nose!' he muttered and stalked out of the room.

When he was gone Flavia breathed a sigh of relief.

'The ball,' she whispered. 'Can you open it, Lupus?'

Lupus nodded and grunted until finally there was a crack and a squeak. He handed Nubia the wooden ball, now in two parts. Inside was a square of parchment, thick and translucent, and lightly powdered with fine chalk dust. One word was written on it in black and gold ink. Nubia took out the parchment and read the word and gasped. Then she held it up for the others to see.

Flavia read the word on the scrap of creamy parchment and her eyes grew wide. '*GLADIATOR*. Nubia, you've won a gladiator!'

SCROLL XVII

'I'm glad my uncle left you behind to stay with us,' said Flavia to Sisyphus, as they set out for the second day's events at the amphitheatre. 'Especially as Caudex still hasn't come back.'

It was early morning, still dark and with a bracing chill in the air.

'I promised to look after you,' said Sisyphus, pulling his deep pink cloak tighter around his shoulders. 'I can't imagine where your bodyguard has disappeared to.'

'He'll show up,' said Flavia. 'Caudex is not very clever but he's very loyal. He probably got lost.'

'By the way,' said Sisyphus, 'as your unofficial guardian, I must ask why you and Lupus are wearing grubby blankets instead of cloaks. And isn't your tunic a bit short?'

Flavia looked at him. 'We worked it all out last night: Lupus is going to pretend to be a slave again and try to find other prison cells. Nubia is going to stay with the beast-fighters; she has a pass. She wanted to bring Tigris but if he barks again, he'll give us away.'

'And you?' said Sisyphus. 'What are your plans?'

Flavia glanced at him. 'I plan to get closer to Fabius, the *magister ludi*. I'm sure he knows who is going to be executed and when.'

'Then I'll be all alone!' Sisyphus gave her an injured look.

'But you can help. You know lots of people in Rome,

other senators and people like that. Pretend you're looking for a friend. Wander around the seats. Find out if anybody knows anything about the prisoners. We're going to meet by the Orpheus fountain at noon, to see what we've found out.'

'Very well,' said Sisyphus and then narrowed his eyes. 'You won't do anything dangerous, will you? The senator would be quite upset if I let anything happen to you.'

'No,' said Flavia, though her heart was pounding. 'I promise it won't be dangerous at all.'

PROGRAMME OF EVENTS

INAUGURAL GAMES DAY II
TO BE HELD AT THE NEW AMPHITHEATRE

EGYPTIAN ACROBATS

EXECUTION OF A CRIMINAL
in which a temple robber will die,
re-enacting the story of Orpheus

BEAST FIGHT
between Pygmies, Crocodiles and Hippos

COMBAT OF NOVELTY GLADIATOR PAIRS
featuring boys & girls

COMBAT OF GLADIATORS

AWNINGS AND DRINKS WILL BE PROVIDED
PRIZES WILL BE DISTRIBUTED

★

Crouching behind a tall umbrella pine, Flavia smeared dust on her face and rubbed it into her hair. She dug her fingernails into the earth at the base of the tree. She knew close examination would show that her hands were soft and manicured and that she had never spent a single day living rough. But the dirt under her fingernails would give an impression of grubbiness. She was betting Fabius didn't have time to carefully interview all the girls for the Orpheus routine.

She was right.

'Did Blastus send you?' he said when she finally stood before him. He was surrounded by slaves, making notes on a four-leafed wax tablet.

'Er … yes.'

'You're an orphan?' He glanced up at her from his tablet.

'Yes,' lied Flavia, and tried to make her lower lip tremble. 'My parents died when I was –'

'Pavo!' barked Fabius, returning his attention to his notes. 'Get this girl to Mater as quickly as possible.' He turned to a scribe: 'Now what were you saying about the Egyptian acrobats?'

Nubia walked into the pungent smell of animals, hay, and dung. It was not long after dawn, so the room was still dim.

'Nubia! Come look at this.' Bar was leaning over a wooden pen. He held a long rod in one hand.

'Hello, Bar.' She joined him on a low ledge around the pen, then gasped as she saw what he was looking at. It was not a pen but a lead-lined, water-filled tank. And it was full of crocodiles.

Instinctively she recoiled at the sight of their evil faces, but Bar smiled and said, 'We're safe here. They can't get out of the tank. Ugly brutes.' He prodded one with his rod. 'The criminal swam right through them last night so they're extra hungry today.'

'I do not think you should be sticking them,' said Nubia. 'You will make them angry.'

He grinned at her, his teeth gleaming white in his smooth brown face. 'That's the idea.'

He jumped down from the ledge of the tank. 'Follow me. I have something else to show you.'

Nubia followed him out of the room through several other dim cells, each housing different caged animals. They passed lions, leopards, ostriches, even a giraffe. In a room with a fawn and several rabbit hutches, Nubia almost tripped over a wooden bucket full of black liquid.

'Careful!' laughed Bar, moving the bucket closer to one of the rabbit hutches. 'If you'd splashed walnut juice on your lionskin it would take ages to come out.'

'Why do you have walnut juice?'

'To dye the rabbits' fur. Otherwise the people on the highest level can't see them against the pale sand.'

Presently they reached another large room with a long tank similar to the first one. Bar helped Nubia up onto the ledge so that she could see into it.

In this tank were half a dozen hippos. Big ones. Their backs and eyes and noses made shiny grey islands in the surface of the water.

Nubia stared at Bar-Mnason in horror.

'My father tells me that of all the animals, the hippo is the most dangerous!' she said.

'Your father's right. Most of the animals here have to be *trained* to attack each other or people. But not the hippos. Put a hippo in the water with a person and they're dead.'

Lupus trailed behind a family with half a dozen children. As they entered one of the arched entrances of the amphitheatre he pushed among them. The real challenge would be getting down into the lower levels.

It wasn't difficult. Nobody wanted to go underground. They all wanted to hurry up to their seats.

Lupus smiled to himself as he slipped through a door and down some dimly lit steps. It was almost too easy.

'You!' growled a man's voice, and at the same instant Lupus felt himself jerked off his feet as a hand gripped the neck of his tunic. 'You're in for it now!'

SCROLL XVIII

Flavia smoothed the pale blue tunic over her thighs. It was very short, and made of the finest silk, gossamer thin. The dim room had a large silver mirror on one wall and she stood for a moment scrutinising her reflection. She had never seen such a big mirror. For the first time in her life she could see herself from head to toe, and very clearly. The woman they called 'Mater' had sent her for a quick scrub in a tank of hot water and three slave-girls had busied themselves over Flavia for half an hour.

Her hair had been brushed and pinned up, then topped with a pink garland woven of peony, crocus and honeysuckle. Her eyes were lined with dark kohl and her cheeks and lips reddened with some bitter tasting paste. Pale blue stibium shimmered on her eyelids. The colour matched her new tunic perfectly and complemented the pink garland. She looked much older than ten. She looked at least thirteen.

Flavia smiled hesitantly at the unfamiliar version of herself in the mirror. Were her knees too knobbly? Was her nose too big? She turned her head and tried to see her profile. She sighed. Her nose did seem to have grown quite a bit in the past few months.

She turned back to face the mirror, and frowned. She was supposed to be a river nymph. What did river nymphs have to do with the legend of Orpheus? She searched the back of her mind and had almost found the answer when suddenly she was jostled to one side.

'Don't spend all day in front of the mirror!'

Flavia turned to see Marcia, the sharp-toothed street urchin. In contrast to Flavia, Marcia wore a tunic of palest pink. Her eyelids were shaded to match and her garland was made of purple crocus and violets, intertwined with honeysuckle.

As the blonde girl preened in front of the mirror Flavia sighed. Marcia's knees were not bumpy. Her nose was pert and pretty and just right. Clean and wearing make-up, the grubby street urchin was beautiful.

Four other girls came chattering into the room, attended by slave-girls who bustled around them, tweaking ribbons, smoothing eyebrows, freshening lip colour. Mater followed the girls in. She was a big woman with large features in a heavily powdered face.

'Time for the show, my beauties!' She clapped her hands.

'What?' squeaked Flavia. 'Already? What about the beast fights? And I haven't found out where they keep the condemned criminals.'

'Shhh!' hissed Marcia fiercely in Flavia's ear. 'You're not allowed to say "criminals" or "executions" or you'll lose us all our gold!'

'What?' said Flavia. 'What are you talking about?'

'Mater told us yesterday. It's one of the rules. If Orpheus plays well today, then he'll be pardoned. So don't mention those words you just said or you'll make him nervous. Look! Here he comes now.'

The man dressed as Orpheus passed close enough for

Flavia to see the strange contrast between his wrinkled face and his dyed black hair.

Flavia lowered her voice. 'But I want to know where they keep the people they're going to ... the prisoners.'

Marcia shook her head, rolled her eyes and turned away.

'Oh my dears!' Mater clasped her meaty hands over her large bosom. 'My dears, you look beautiful. Simply beautiful. So young and tender. Proper little river nymphs ...' She wiped her eye.

'Now!' she said briskly. 'Into the boat with you. You're to row Orpheus to the island as he plays his beautiful music. You all practised last night ... well, all except for you ...' she turned to Flavia. 'Presumably you can follow their lead? And you know how to hold an oar, I hope?'

'Of course,' said Flavia. 'My father is – er ... I mean, before I was tragically orphaned, my father was a sea captain.'

'How nice for you, dear. Now, everybody up the stairs and into the boat. Remember, blue tunics on the left and pink tunics on the right.'

'May we keep the tunics after we've finished?' asked a girl of about twelve.

'Of course,' said Mater. 'And your sacks of gold will be here when you come back.'

The bald slave called Blastus led them up the stairs and as Flavia followed she heard the girls chattering about what they would spend their money on. Presently they all emerged into a room with marble walls and a bright opening straight ahead. A thick layer of sawdust covered the floor, and on the sawdust a splash of some dark reddish-brown liquid.

Flavia's step faltered and she gazed down at the ominous stain.

'Don't worry, dear,' said Mater, who had followed them up and who was dry-eyed and businesslike again. She gave Flavia a firm push. 'One of the slaves must have had a little accident earlier.'

'But that looks like –'

'Into the boat, dears! Orpheus is waiting.'

Mater hustled Flavia forward. Blastus took her arm and suddenly she felt herself being lifted out into the immense bright space of the arena and down into a pretty gilded boat draped with garlands of peony, violet and saffron.

'Sit here at the back,' said Blastus. He indicated a pale blue cushion covering a plank seat in the boat. Flavia was the last girl in. A moment later the ship wobbled as the bald slave stepped out of it and back up into the arch. He gave them a good push with a boat hook.

As the boat slid smoothly forward, Flavia gripped her pink oar, looked over her shoulder and gasped. The sandy arena had been transformed into a mirror-bright lake with a lovely green island at its centre.

'When did they do that?' she murmured.

'Last night,' said Marcia behind her.

'Don't talk. Row!' Orpheus spoke for the first time. 'The Emperor's brother has promised me a total reprieve if we perform well.' He was dressed in a pure white tunic and golden sandals. 'And sing!' He strummed his gilded lyre.

But Flavia and the other girls stared around, dumbfounded. Even if they had been able to utter a squeak they would not have been heard. For as the boat moved into view, a deafening roar filled the vast interior of the amphitheatre.

Fifty thousand Romans were cheering the pretty blonde girls in the gilded boat.

Flavia gulped. Fifty thousand Romans were cheering her!

'You!' growled the big man, and Lupus relaxed as he recognised Verucus's ugly face looming over him.

Lupus gave the man a sheepish smile.

'Don't grin at me like that!' Verucus cuffed Lupus on the head. 'Where were you yesterday? Watching the games no doubt! Well, your punishment today will be fitting. You can empty latrine buckets!'

Lupus sighed, and trudged after the big slave. Presently his spirits lifted: they were going to a part of the arena he hadn't been to before. That meant there were other prisoners being held in this part of the amphitheatre. Jonathan might be among them.

'Look at that!' Verucus pointed to water soaking the floor. 'They flooded the arena last night. It's supposed to be watertight but it isn't. Half the prisoners are up to their ankles in water. It was Titus and Domitian's bright idea for the shows last night and this morning. But it's not working. I've already heard rumours that they're going to forget the waterworks and put in cells like the ones at Capua, so the animals can appear in the arena as if by magic. Here we are. Orpheus's cell.'

Verucus lifted the thick oak bar and pushed open the heavy door. Lupus wrinkled his nose as he stepped in. The empty cell was dark and smelly. There was no furniture, only a plaster-covered sleeping shelf along one wall and a wooden bucket in the corner. At one end of the sleeping couch lay an iron chain with an empty leg-manacle on the end.

'Grab the latrine bucket!' growled Verucus. 'This one isn't coming back; we can take it with us.'

He bolted the door after Lupus and shook his head sadly. 'The prisoner in the next cell is just a boy. They say he started the fire last month.'

Lupus's heart thumped. Was it Jonathan? He knew he was about to find out.

'Are these hippos for the beast fight?' Nubia asked Bar Mnason. 'How will they move the heavy tanks to where people can see?'

'They won't move the tanks.' He laughed. 'You haven't seen the amphitheatre today, have you?'

Nubia shook her head.

'They flooded it with water last night for a show of nereids, a mock sea-battle and an execution. All done by torchlight. The water's five feet deep. Same depth as the water in this tank.' He laughed at the expression on her face. 'The acrobats were swinging over it earlier and the tightrope walkers are on now. Let's hope the elephant doesn't fall in. That would make one big splash!' He laughed. 'See that door there, at the end of the tank?'

Nubia nodded.

'When we open it the hippos and crocs will be able to swim right into the arena. And the water is so clear that even the ladies on the top level will be able to see them.'

'Then the hippos and crocs will do water beast fight?' asked Nubia.

'Much better than that,' said Bar-Mnason with a grin.

'Come here.'

He led her to a slit in the gently curving marble wall. 'Look through this viewing slit. It's almost invisible to people in the stands but it means we can see what's happening out in the arena.'

Nubia put her eye to the horizontal crack. Her view was restricted, and at first she couldn't tell what she was looking at. She could see a double tier of almost identical seats. Then she gasped. The arena was full of water, and rows of white-togaed senators were reflected in its glassy surface. The water was unbroken except where an island reared up in the middle.

'Behold! I mean: look! An island!'

'It's good, isn't it? Made of wood, covered with dirt, shrubs and trees. There's even a cave. They used it last night for the naval battle and execution. Except the criminal survived,' he said, and added, 'I told them we should have put in the hippos.'

'How do they find so much water?'

'Channelled down from the aqueduct. Only took a few hours to fill before the night show.' He gestured with his chin. 'Father's in the island now. With the caged bears.'

'I do not see him on the island.'

'I didn't say "on" the island. I said "in" the island.'

'Why is he in the island?'

'For the Orpheus routine.'

Nubia turned away from the viewing slit to look up at Bar.

'Why is a criminal being dressed as Orpheus?'

Bar shrugged. 'The Romans like to publicly execute criminals and entertain the crowds at the same time.

They're efficient.'

'But Orpheus was a musician who played beautiful music, so beautiful as to charm trees and stones and fierce animals.' Nubia brought her eye to the slit again. 'So why is a criminal being dressed as Orpheus?'

Bar shrugged. 'Who knows? Maybe the man was a musician. Or maybe he's from Thrace, like Orpheus. The Romans don't really need a reason. They love the Greek myths more than the Greeks.' Bar chuckled. 'Orpheus is going to be rowed to the island by beautiful blonde girls.'

Nubia nodded to herself. Flavia had told them the night before about this routine. She hoped to take part in it so that she could ask Fabius about the prisoners.

'There are already some tame animals on the island,' Bar was saying, 'but half way through his second song my father will release the bears. Then we'll see if "Orpheus" can charm the animals with his music!'

Nubia's heart stuttered as she realised what he was saying. 'Bears?' she cried. 'Alas, the girls will be in terrible danger!'

SCROLL XIX

'The girls are in danger!' Nubia gripped Bar-Mnason's arm.

'What? Do you mean those little blonde water nymphs?'

'Yes!'

He laughed. 'Those bears won't hurt the girls. They'll be too busy eating Orpheus.'

'Oh.' Nubia felt sick with relief.

'No, the bears won't eat the girls,' he repeated, as he slid open the door of the tank. 'That's what these beauties are for.'

'What?'

Bar nodded. 'It was Domitian's idea. That's why he told Fabius to choose girls less than five feet tall, all slaves and orphans. If they don't drown, the hippos and crocs will get them.'

'No!' cried Nubia. 'NO!'

'What is it? They're only slaves.'

'One of them is my friend Flavia!'

'One of the nymphs is your friend?'

Nubia nodded. 'Don't let hippos out!'

'Too late,' said Bar. 'There they go.' He cursed under his breath.

'We must do something!' Nubia clutched his arm. 'Bar, I must go out there to help her!'

He shook his head grimly. 'You can only get to the

island when the arena is dry, not when it's full of water. I'm sorry, Nubia. Your friend is doomed.'

Flavia grinned in delight as wave after wave of cheering washed over her.

The girls had got over their initial surprise and were now rowing in unison, the pretty oars flashing pink and blue as the boat moved out over the placid water towards the green island. Orpheus was strumming and as the cheers gradually subsided he began to sing.

The girls sang 'La, la-la-la, la-laa!' and the water organ played the same tune, but softly so that the girls could be heard. People in the upper tiers had caught the tune and started to sing the 'la-la' part along with the girls.

The scent of honeysuckle suddenly filled Flavia's head and at the same moment an equally sweet sensation filled her chest. It was an emotion she had never felt before, a complex mixture of pleasure, excitement and self-consciousness.

Was this what Fame felt like? Or was it Glory?

Whatever it was, she liked it.

She glanced over her shoulder and saw that they were nearly at the island. Presently the boat nudged the land and Orpheus leapt nimbly onto the grassy turf.

Two of the girls at the front used their oars to push the boat away from the island and they began to row languidly round the island.

Orpheus placed one foot on a painted rock and sang the story of how his wife Eurydice was bitten by a poisonous viper on the very day of their wedding. He sang of how he was willing to visit death to bring her back.

His voice hardly quavered as he sang of how he, Orpheus, was going to descend to the underworld, charm Cerberus with his music and melt the hearts of Pluto and Persephone.

'Then I will bring Eurydice back,' he sang, 'bring my true love back from death!'

'Oooh!' said the crowd, as a dozen colourful birds fluttered out of the cave mouth and settled on the small trees and shrubs around Orpheus.

'Aaaaah!' they sighed a moment later, as some white rabbits hopped out, followed by a dappled, long-legged fawn.

' Wha – !' The sharp intake of breath in fifty thousand Roman throats was one of the strangest sounds Flavia had ever heard. She looked over her shoulder to see a dark shape emerging from the cave mouth.

'Bear!' one of the girls behind her screamed. 'There's a bear on the island!'

Orpheus's tremolo became a strangled squeal.

Flavia and the other girls stopped pulling their oars.

Orpheus's eyes bulged in terror and although his mouth was open, no sound emerged.

As soon as he ran, the bear began to pursue him.

'Here!' he gasped, shoving the fawn into the bear's path. 'Eat this!'

But the bear must have been trained to crave human flesh. The huge creature ignored the tottering fawn and lumbered after Orpheus.

The amphitheatre resounded with waves of laughter as the bear chased Orpheus round the little island. Above the laughter Flavia heard catcalls drift down from the upper levels.

'Eurydice has sent you a gift from the underworld,' someone joked.

'Use your lyre, Orpheus!'

'Charm him with your music!'

'Don't throw it! Play it!'

'Serves you right for robbing the temple!'

Suddenly – too late – Flavia remembered where river nymphs appeared in the story of Orpheus.

After his death, they had found his lyre, his dismembered limbs and his head.

Some of the girls in the boat were laughing now too, but Flavia could see the look of pure terror on the man's face and something brown, presumably hair dye, dripping down his forehead with the sweat. She knew what must happen to him.

'Jump in the water!' Flavia shouted at him. 'Jump!'

But Orpheus kept running. Perhaps he hadn't heard her, or maybe he couldn't swim.

Suddenly there was a thunderous cheer and Marcia pointed towards the cave. 'Another bear!' she laughed. 'Now he'll get it!'

Some of the girls were crying and some were laughing, but not one of them was rowing. The boat drifted slowly away from the island.

The crowd roared as the biggest bear finally brought down Orpheus with a swipe of his paw. As the two big creatures loomed over the fallen man Flavia averted her eyes. Presently she blocked her ears, too, in order to drown out his screams.

A sharp elbow in Flavia's ribs forced her fingers out of her ears for a moment.

'Look!' said Marcia. 'One of the bears has his arm!'

She giggled but suddenly her giggle turned to a scream. 'Our boat!' she cried, pointing down. 'It's sinking!'

Flavia looked down. Two inches of water lapped around her bare feet at the bottom of the boat. She had been so upset by the terrible scene on the island that she hadn't even noticed. Now – even as she watched – she saw a crack widen in the bottom of the boat and a terrible thought struck her.

'What if Orpheus wasn't the only one who had been tricked?' she said.

But nobody heard her. The other girls were beginning to scream and cry for help. Flavia glanced up towards the Imperial Box. Titus would help them.

But the man sitting in the Emperor's chair was not Titus. He was younger, with brown hair. He was laughing, saying something to the woman next to him and pointing at them.

Domitian.

It was the Emperor's younger brother Domitian.

And he wasn't pointing at the sinking boat. He was pointing *beyond* it.

Flavia slowly stood in the boat and looked back.

'The boat's sinking!' screamed Marcia hysterically. 'I can't swim and the boat's sinking! We're all going to drown!'

'No,' said Flavia in a trembling voice, 'we won't drown. Those hippos will get us first.'

SCROLL XX

Sound receded from Flavia, so that the cries of the crowds and the surge of the water organ and the screams of the girls in the boat were barely audible. She had seen hippos in mosaics and Nubia had told her what these huge creatures could do.

Everything seemed to happen very slowly. Two of the girls were trying to paddle back the way they had come, the others were standing, making the fragile boat rock violently. The water was up to Flavia's ankles now and a girl's terrified face loomed into view. It was Marcia, screaming something, shaking Flavia by the shoulders.

But all Flavia could hear was the roaring of blood in her ears.

Suddenly she felt rather than heard the boat crack. It split neatly in two. Flavia gasped at the shock of the cold water but managed to close her mouth a moment before it closed over her head. Her toes brushed the sandy bottom so she pushed herself back up.

Sobbing for breath and dragging the wet hair from her eyes, she began to tread water and look around. They were all in the water now. The boat was in pieces around them, oars and garlands floating, the girls thrashing.

A hand clutched at her arm, hurting her with the tightness of its grip: Marcia's terrified face, eyes rolling, teeth bared. Then Marcia was wrenched violently away from Flavia as a hippo took her in his terrible jaws.

Water filled Flavia's screaming mouth. She rose up, coughing. Out of the corner of her eye, she saw a second hippo drag one of the other girls under.

The island. She must get to the island. It was her only hope. Her heart was pounding so hard she thought she would die, but she kicked out for the island and swam. Thank the gods Lupus had taught her how to swim last summer. She concentrated on her breathing and her strokes, trying not to think about what she had just seen.

Presently she noticed the water around her was pink, but she tried not to think about that either.

Now every breath was an effort because her chest was tight with fear. Her legs and arms were trembling but she swam doggedly for the island. Not far now.

Over to her right, a log floated in the water. She veered towards that. If she could just reach it and hang on for a moment she could get her bearings and catch her breath. She was almost there when the log opened one evil yellow eye and turned with a flick of its terrible tail.

Flavia found herself staring into the opening jaws of a crocodile.

'The prisoner in this cell is only a boy,' said Verucus to Lupus. 'They say he started the fire last month but it's obvious the lad wouldn't hurt a fly. Poor lad. He has no idea what's in store for him.'

Verucus slid back the bolt, pushed open the cell door and attempted a cheerful greeting: 'Good morning, Curly-top! We've come to empty your latrine bucket and

I've brought you a nice white roll for your breakfast.'

Lupus's heart was pounding. Jonathan. It had to be Jonathan!

As he stepped into the dim cell his eyes widened at the sight of a boy with dark, curly hair stretched out on the sleeping shelf.

Flavia had once heard that when you are about to die your past life unrolls before you like a painted scroll. But as she stared down the throat of the crocodile she did not see her life unscroll.

She saw her father's face. What would he do without her? He would be so sad. He had lost too many people. No! She refused to die!

She looked around for something to use as a weapon. An oar. A piece of wood from the boat. Anything. But there was only a purple garland floating on the pink water.

The crocodile had closed its mouth to move forward through the water.

Suddenly Flavia had an idea. She grasped the garland and instead of swimming away from the crocodile she swam straight towards it. Before it could open its terrible jaws again she thrust the garland over its snout and then rolled away and kicked out furiously for the island.

Even above the sound of her beating heart and the splash of her arms in the water she could hear the roar of the crowd. She dared not look behind her. The garland was made of violets, crocuses and honeysuckle threaded onto a hemp cord. It might gain her a little more time. But not much.

She was at the island now, but as she clawed at the

grass bank above her, a chunk of turf detached itself and fell away. Then another. There was no handhold.

Flavia tried to pull herself up again and again, but now her arms were trembling and she was beginning to sob. She had failed. She knew the crocodile's yellow teeth would sink into her legs any moment, dragging her down to a terrible death.

'Flavia!' cried a familiar voice from above her. 'Behold! I am here.'

Suddenly dark brown hands gripped her wrists and Flavia felt herself being lifted up and up, out of the water, into the cool air.

She was flying!

Above her was Nubia's beautiful, grave face, framed by the lion's head of her cloak. Below her was the huge crocodile, rising up out of the water and snapping at her feet.

But his jaws shut on empty air as the two girls swung back over the island.

The crowd went wild.

The demigod Hercules had descended from Olympus to save the brave young river nymph.

'Let go!' gasped Nubia. 'I am not being so strong as to hold you for the ride back up.'

Flavia nodded and let go. She fell a few feet and rolled on the grassy turf of the man-made island, sending rabbits hopping away.

Holding the rope with her right hand, Nubia undid the clasp of the harness with her left and dropped down after her friend.

It had taken all Nubia's self-control not to faint as they

had lowered her from a hundred and fifty feet up. She had hoped to help some of the other girls but by the time she reached the island she knew Flavia was the only one still alive.

Now, remembering what she had seen on her way down, Nubia knelt on the grass and vomited.

She looked up and saw a shivering Flavia standing with her hand outstretched. Nubia let herself be pulled to her feet and then shrugged off her lionskin cloak.

'You wear it,' she said, wrapping it around her friend's shoulders. 'You are shivering and cold and your tunic is see-through when wet.'

'Quick, girls!' said a man's voice. 'Get in the cave. Those bears have been trained to crave human flesh. If they smell you ...'

Nubia nodded and took Flavia's arm. She averted her eyes from the bloody arm on the grass and pulled her friend towards the mouth of the cave.

Suddenly she froze. One of the bears had appeared round the hillock, walking on its hind legs like a person. Nubia's blood ran cold. It was a Nubian bear, the biggest and fiercest of all bears. Blood dripped from its paws and muzzle and its chest was matted with it. The bear paused and stood swaying, testing the air with its bloody nose.

Flavia drew a deep breath to scream but Nubia dug her fingers into her friend's arm.

'Never show an animal that you fear it!' she said quietly.

Flavia closed her mouth and nodded. She was trembling so much that Nubia could feel her body shaking.

'In here!' came the voice from the cave, and Nubia

recognised it as Mnason's.

But now the bear was between them and the cave mouth. Its uplifted nose caught their scent and slowly it turned towards them.

Nubia thought quickly. Could she calm it with a song? Her instinct said no, so she spoke, calmly but loudly, 'Go away, bear!'

The bear swayed, almost imperceptibly.

Nubia knew it wasn't hungry – it had just been gorging on Orpheus – and she had used her most commanding voice. For one brief moment she thought her plan had worked.

Then the bear's evil little eyes glinted as it dropped on all fours and charged straight at them.

Lupus felt a huge surge of hope fill his chest as the curly-haired boy lifted himself from the sleeping couch and turned to face them.

Then his spirits plunged. Even in the dim light of the cell, he could see the boy was not Jonathan. This boy had delicate features, pale eyes and an odd smile.

'Hello, Verucus,' said the boy. 'How are you?' His voice was high, lilting, almost girlish.

'I'm fine, sunshine!' said Verucus. 'Lupus here is going to empty your latrine bucket.'

'Hello, Lupus,' said the boy with a sweet smile.

Lupus barely glanced at him. He felt tears prick his eyes and he swallowed a sob that threatened to tear away his pride.

This was the curly-haired boy they had been looking for all this time. And it was not Jonathan. It was just a blue-eyed simpleton.

SCROLL XXI

As the bear loped towards them, Flavia closed her eyes and gripped Nubia's hand. She would not scream. If she had to die at least she would die bravely.

Suddenly she heard the crowd utter a thunderous cheer and she opened her eyes. The bear had staggered to a stop. Then she saw the arrow protruding from its shaggy side. Even as she watched, it received a second arrow in the neck. Another roar from the crowd.

The first bear was down, but now the second had appeared. Immediately it, too, received two arrows in the head.

Flavia turned to see who was firing the arrows; they seemed to be coming from the stands.

'There!' whispered Nubia, and pointed.

Flavia followed her finger and her jaw dropped.

The arrows were coming from the Imperial Box.

Another arrow, and as the second bear finally collapsed, the crowd erupted in a deafening cheer.

The archer laid aside his bow and waved at the girls.

They were safe. Alive and safe. Flavia felt her knees trembling violently and now everything was speeding away from her and she knew even Nubia wouldn't be able to hold her up.

But just before she fainted Flavia managed to wave

weakly back at their saviour, the Emperor's younger brother. Domitian.

'Oh!' groaned Flavia. 'What happened?' She tasted wine and felt the hard leather nozzle of the wineskin against her teeth.

'Drink this.' The voice was familiar.

'I'm going to be sick.'

'Drink the wine, it helps.' Nubia's voice.

Flavia drank the undiluted wine and looked around.

She was in a dim, dank space made of wood and plaster.

'Nubia,' she said, and hugged her friend. Nubia was wearing her lionskin again and Flavia had a prickly blanket wrapped round her. It smelt faintly of dung and some musky animal smell.

Then she saw white teeth gleaming in a dusky face. 'Mnason!'

He nodded. 'Hello, Flavia Gemina. You were amazing. Putting your garland around the croc's mouth: that was inspired.'

'You saw that?'

He nodded. 'Peephole there. Above the waterline. We're inside the island, by the way. I wanted to help you but I was too far away. And you, Nubia! How did you get up to the top so quickly? And how did you convince the slaves to lower you on the rope?'

'Your son,' said Nubia. 'He commands slaves to help me and he shows me how to do and undo clasp.'

'Clever boy. And brave girl.'

'Can we go now?' whimpered Flavia. Despite the blanket, she was shivering uncontrollably.

Mnason shook his head. 'Sorry,' he said. 'Not yet.'

Flavia heard a muffled cheer.

'What's happening?' she asked, trying not to think about what she had just seen.

'They've started to drain the water and they've sent in pygmies to kill off the crocs and hippos.'

'What is a pygmy?'

'A race of very small people from Africa.'

'Oh. Can we go now?'

'There's no way out of here while the water is still in the arena. Only if it's dry. When the water's drained away, they'll roll us off and we can get out of here.' He paused and Flavia saw his teeth flash again as he grinned. 'I don't suppose you girls would like to join the pygmies out there?' he said. 'The crowd would love it and I could promise you a bag of gold each ...'

'No thanks,' groaned Flavia, 'I think we've had enough excitement for one day.'

'His imperial majesty, Titus Flavius Domitianus!' announced the soldier and gently pushed Nubia and Flavia forward.

It was almost noon and the girls had been summoned to take a light lunch with their saviour Domitian. In the Imperial Box a dozen interested faces turned towards them.

'Thetis the sea nymph and Hercules the hero!' exclaimed Domitian, rising from an elaborately carved ivory chair and coming towards them. 'But now I can see it's Hercula. You're no boy!'

The Emperor's younger brother was not tall, but he was muscular and good-looking, with curly brown hair and large brown eyes. Nubia felt her face grow hot under his gaze and she dropped her eyes.

'Caesar,' murmured Flavia, she moved forward and shakily kissed Domitian's outstretched hand. Nubia followed her example.

Domitian lifted Nubia to her feet and she heard the quaver in Flavia's voice as her friend said: 'Thank you for saving our lives.'

'You are very welcome. I enjoyed it. I'm an excellent archer and I never miss an opportunity to show off.'

Nubia darted a quick glance up at him and then quickly lowered her gaze.

He was still looking straight at her.

SCROLL XXII

'Sit, girls!' said the Emperor's younger brother, gesturing towards a cushioned couch to the left of his throne at the very front of the box. As he spoke a long-haired slave-boy set a light table before it. 'We're about to take some refreshment.'

'Flavia! Nubia!' cried a voice from the entrance. 'Great Juno's peacock! Are you girls all in one piece?'

Nubia saw Sisyphus struggling to push his way between two burly guards.

'Oh Sisyphus!' cried Flavia. She ran to the slim Greek and threw her arms round him.

Domitian raised an eyebrow. 'Is this your father?'

'Caesar!' Sisyphus's eyes grew wide and Nubia saw him try to bow with Flavia still clinging to him. 'Caesar, my name is Sisyphus. I am secretary to Senator Cornix. His niece Flavia Gemina and her friend Nubia are under my protection.'

'Charmed to meet you. Do come in and join us.' Domitian spread himself comfortably back in his ivory chair. 'This is my wife Domitia,' – he lazily waved an arm to his right – 'my niece Julia and her husband Flavius Sabinus. Also my friends Calvus the senator and Martial, a poet.'

'Oh Sisyphus, it was terrible!' said Flavia. 'First the hippos, and then the crocodiles, and then the bear...'

Nubia heard Flavia's teeth chattering.

'I know! My dear, If I hadn't seen it I wouldn't have believed it. But the crowds loved it. Come, let's accept Caesar's kind offer and sit here on the couch beside Nubia the heroine! Are you all right, my dear?' This last to Nubia.

She nodded and gave him a weak smile.

'Nubia ex machina,' said Sisyphus. 'My dear, you were superb!'

Beside her Flavia was still trembling so violently that the whole couch was shaking.

Nubia took Mnason's scratchy blanket from her friend's shoulders and replaced it with a soft blue cover from the imperial couch.

'Take some refreshment.' Domitian was watching them. 'Go on, Nubia-the-heroine, I command it!' he laughed.

Nubia obediently leaned forward and took a date from the low table. As she bit into its delicious chewy sweetness, she suddenly realised that she was ravenously hungry.

Suspended in space above the arena, midgets were having lunch, too. They sat on chairs balanced on the tightrope and they tossed fruit back and forth while the water organ played a jolly tune. Below them, slaves were running to bring the last sections of wooden planking to cover the now empty basin. Nubia was amazed at how much bigger and more detailed everything was from the this level.

She turned her attention to the other occupants of the box, and as Domitian and his guests began to eat, she secretly studied them.

Domitian's wife Domitia was a dark-haired woman, with a strong nose and a weak chin. Her complicated hairdo was so stiff and her posture so rigid that she might have been carved of marble. In complete contrast, Domitian's niece Julia made Nubia think of a ripe peach. She was a pretty redhead of about fourteen or fifteen. She had a short neck, a plump body and a mouth shaped like Cupid's bow. Nubia noticed that Julia kept glancing towards Domitian, and once she saw him wink back at her.

Sitting on one side of Julia was a pleasant-looking man with reddish-brown hair, presumably her husband. On Julia's other side sat an ape-like man with hairy arms and legs, and eyebrows that met over his nose. He was taking notes on a wax tablet. A bald man wearing a red-striped tunic had vacated their couch to sit in a gilded chair behind them. He must be the senator.

Slave-boys came into the box carrying silver trays with little pastry animals on them. Flavia shook her head as Sisyphus coaxingly pressed a honey and almond hippo against her firmly-closed mouth. It was obvious to Nubia that her friend had no appetite.

But Nubia had never felt hungrier and when the slave-boy extended the tray to her, she devoured three lions, two tigers and a bear.

Lupus sought a hiding place where nobody could find him.

He had ignored Verucus's bellow of rage to run blindly through one dim corridor after another. Finally he had found this high little niche, behind a statue of Cupid. It was tight and he had to bend his head but somehow it felt safe. He felt like an injured animal who has crept back to its lair to lick its wounds. But his wounds were inside and the only way to soothe them was to weep. So he let the great hot tears pour silently down his cheeks.

Everything had depended on the curly-haired boy of the rumours being Jonathan. But the boy was not Jonathan. That meant Jonathan must be dead.

There was no hope left.

Nubia leaned on the marble parapet and gazed out over the arena.

'Where once was water now is dry land,' she heard the hairy-armed man proclaim.

'Virgil?' asked Domitian.

'My own verse,' said the poet, looking smug. 'I have just composed it.'

'Very good,' everyone murmured, and Nubia nodded, too.

It was hard to believe that the place where five girls her age had just died was sand again, clean and pure. As clean and pure as the desert, the golden desert of her child-hood.

Would she ever be able to see sand again without thinking of pain and death? Without wondering how deep she would have to dig to find blood? Had the Romans made it impossible for her to go home again?

She gazed up at the thousands of people in the vast bowl around her. What was she doing here?

Trying to find Jonathan, she told herself. I'm here to find Jonathan.

Jonathan, who had been closer than a brother since the night the four of them had swum with dolphins. Jonathan, who bound them together with his steady friendship the way the deep bass notes of his barbiton brought together their flute, drums and tambourine.

If Jonathan was no longer there to hold them together then she must do it. Flavia and Lupus had become her new family. And she could not afford to lose another family. It was up to her to keep them together and to protect them.

'Nubia,' she heard a voice whisper behind her and turned to see Flavia extending her hand. With a smile Nubia took it and sat beside her friend and comforted her as she wept.

And for the first time since they had met, Nubia felt she was stronger than Flavia.

Lupus's tears were subsiding when he heard voices and approaching footsteps. He sniffed and wiped his nose on his finger. Then he froze.

'The senators are outraged by the murder of those little girls.' A man's voice – low and urgent – and speaking Greek.

His companion – a man with a deeper voice – replied in the same language. 'That parade of informers yesterday meant nothing. This morning Titus showed his true nature. We said he'd be a second Nero, and it looks as if we were right.'

'You know, my friend. This could be the perfect time for us to do what we've spoken of before … to take his throne. But we must act immediately.'

SCROLL XXIII

Lupus wiped the tears from his cheeks and slowly leaned forward to see the two men whispering in the corridor below him. If he peered under the marble cupid's chubby arm, he could just see them. The one with the deeper voice had a bald patch. The other one was very tall and thin. They were in their early thirties, he guessed, and the broad red stripes on their white tunics told him that they were of the senatorial class.

'You and I?' said Bald Patch. 'Co-rulers instead of Titus and Domitian?'

'Why not?' said the tall one. 'We've discussed this before. We're both of better ancestry. You come from the Julian line and my great-grandmother was Pompey's niece. Their father was a mule-driving farmer from the Sabine Hills.'

'And you think now is the time?'

'Now is the perfect time. The slaughter of those little girls was outrageous. We'll start speaking to the senators today. Test the –'

'Shhh! Did you hear something?'

Lupus moved back into the shadows and held his breath.

'Let's go outside,' said Bald Patch. 'No risk of being heard there.'

Lupus heard their footsteps retreating and presently all was quiet, except for the distant roar of the crowds.

He knew he had to make a decision.

Titus's throne was at risk. The Emperor's life might even be in danger.

But only yesterday Titus had flogged Rome's informers and then paraded them in the arena.

Lupus knew that if he told Titus about the plot, it would make him just like them. He would be an informer, too.

'What is the meaning of this?' a bellowing voice rose up the stairs and filled the Imperial Box.

Nubia looked up to see the Emperor Titus appear. He was gripping his purple cloak in one hand and the man called Fabius in the other. Titus flung away the cloak in a swirl of purple and forced the *magister ludi* to his knees on the coloured marble floor.

'Freeborn girls being fed to hippos? Ten-year-olds fighting off crocodiles? What in Hades did you think you were doing?' The Emperor's face was flushed with rage. 'I parade a thousand informers to snuff out the rumour that I will be another Nero, and what do you do? You follow it up with a show of little blonde girls that even that depraved maniac would not have dreamed of!'

Fabius hung his head.

Titus was still breathing hard but now his face was returning to its normal colour. He pulled out his handkerchief and mopped his brow.

'Well? What do you have to say for yourself?'

Fabius lifted his head. 'Caesar, forgive me. The girls ...

We thought it would please the crowds. It *did* please the crowds. They were only slaves ...'

'Not all of them, as I understand it,' said Titus. 'I have been informed that some were freeborn and that one in particular was of the equestrian class.'

'Imposs–,' began Fabius, and his eyes widened as he caught sight of a red-eyed Flavia shivering on her couch.

Titus turned to follow Fabius's gaze and his eyes widened, too.

'Flavia Gemina!' he said and his eyebrows went up. 'Were you part of that outrage?'

Flavia nodded, and then burst into fresh tears. Nubia patted her shoulder.

Fabius scrambled to his feet. 'But Caesar, your brother Domitian approved today's programme. And that girl swore she was an orphan –'

'Silence!' bellowed Titus and pointed at Flavia. 'This girl saved my life last year. If she had died ...' he took a breath and lowered his voice to a menacing whisper, '... if she had died, then your fate would have been sealed. As it is ... I'll give you a chance. Among the gladiators you love so dearly.'

'But, Caesar!' Fabius whimpered.

'Take him!' Titus gave two soldiers a curt nod and they hustled Fabius out of the Imperial Box.

Titus turned to Domitian, 'You knew of this?'

Domitian had vacated the imperial throne and was reclining on a couch. He gave his older brother a lazy shrug. 'Fabius and I thought it would make the execution more entertaining ...'

'Entertaining?' spluttered Titus, then he took a deep

breath and tried to steady his voice. 'Yes,' he said patiently, as if speaking to a child. 'The executions are meant to entertain the masses. But also to educate them. And to discourage them from committing similar crimes. Above all, Domitian,' he raised his voice so that the senators around him would be able to hear, 'above all, the executions must show justice being done.'

Domitian took an olive. 'You pardoned that so-called Leander last night after he swam through the crocodiles.'

'It is my duty to show mercy on occasion. Besides, if the gods spared him, he must have been unjustly accused. Pardoning someone who may be innocent is a different matter from condemning those who have done no wrong. The only crime those poor little girls were guilty of was in being lowborn. And one of them was highborn. We should never submit those of noble birth to this kind of humiliation!'

Domitian gestured at Flavia. 'Well, I saved the high-born one, didn't I?'

'You very nearly didn't, by all reports,' muttered Titus and glanced round the box. 'Domitian. You and I will discuss this further in private. But now please return to the Palatine. I'll oversee the gladiator combats.'

Domitian rose slowly to his feet and inclined his head. 'Very well, Caesar,' he said. 'Come, Domitia.' And although he sauntered down the stairs out of the Imperial Box with every appearance of calm Nubia knew better.

She had seen the look of pure hatred in his eyes when he looked at Titus.

'Excuse me, Caesar!' said a broken-nosed guard, stepping forward. 'There's a boy here who claims to have information about a plot against you. I would have tossed him out but he assures me that you know him.' The big guard extended a battered wax tablet.

'An informer?' Titus closed his eyes, pinched the top of his nose and sighed deeply. 'I didn't think there were any left in Rome after yesterday. Well, let's see.' He took the tablet, opened it and examined it. From her couch beside him, Flavia caught a glimpse of two portraits etched in the wax.

'Ah!' He sat up straight and glanced up at the guard. 'I've suspected these two for some time. Arrest them at once. And show the boy in, would you?'

The guard went out and returned a moment later with a dark-haired boy in a grubby tunic.

'Lupus!' exclaimed Flavia, Nubia and Sisyphus.

If Lupus was surprised to see his friends in the Imperial Box he did not show it. He gave them a dull look.

'You discovered a plot against the Emperor?' asked Flavia, and for a moment her shivering subsided.

He nodded.

Titus put his hand on Lupus's shoulder. 'Come,' he said, 'sit and have something to eat ... or to drink. Then I want you to tell me how you found out about Africanus and Stertinius. You can stay here in my box for rest of the afternoon. There's no better seat in the amphitheatre. The best part of the show is about to begin: the gladiatorial combats.'

'Did you find …?' Flavia started to whisper as Lupus joined them on the couch. But she trailed off. His bleak expression said it all. He didn't even have to shake his head for Flavia to know he had not found Jonathan.

Flavia leaned her head on Nubia's shoulder. Even with the warm imperial blanket wrapped around her she was shivering more than ever.

A silver cup of cool spiced wine and the trumpets' blare raised Lupus's spirits a little. He leaned forward as the gladiators emerged into the bright arena from an entrance to his right.

'Are they starting already?' Titus put down his plate and glanced up at the sun. 'It seems too early.'

The crowd was cheering and laughing. People who had left to buy midday snacks or visit the latrines were hurrying back to their seats.

'It's the novelty act, Caesar,' said Calvus, the bald senator.

Lupus glanced out into the arena again.

The gladiators wore their armour and carried their helmets so the crowd could see their faces. Behind came their attendants, carrying weapons, and finally the lanista.

'Novelty act?' said Titus.

'Yes,' said Calvus. 'You remember that female gladiators fought yesterday afternoon?'

Just outside the Imperial Box some senators were making exclamations of outrage.

'Yes?' said Titus. 'But those aren't women.'

Lupus sat up straight and looked harder. Then his eyes widened.

'No,' said Calvus, 'your brother arranged something quite new for today's show. He thought the crowds might be amused –'

But before he could finish Lupus heard the Emperor exclaim.

'They're children!'

SCROLL XXIV

As the fanfare died away, an announcer walked onto the sandy oval of the arena and looked up at the Imperial Box. Flavia could hear him perfectly.

'For your amusement and pleasure,' he proclaimed, 'five pairs of child gladiators will now do combat.'

Flavia pulled her blue blanket tighter and sat up straight.

As the young gladiators paired off and began warming up with wooden weapons, she saw that some were girls her age.

'According to lots cast earlier,' announced the herald, 'the pairing will be as follows: Hostis and Prometheus: a Murmillo versus a Thracian. Serpens and Bastet, a hoplomachus and a fish-girl. Two matches between secutor and retiarius: first will be Flaccus and Oceanus, next will be Ursus and Numerius. But to begin today's novelty bouts we have Vulpina, fighting as secutrix, against Mus the net-girl.'

'Ahhhh!' sighed the crowd as the herald indicated a tiny girl with a wooden trident. She wore nothing but a loincloth and the distinctive arm padding and shoulder guard of the net-man.

Nubia gazed at Flavia with dismay. 'She is so young!'

Lupus held up eight fingers.

'Maybe younger,' said Flavia.

Titus had risen from his throne and was gripping the marble balustrade with white-knuckled hands. Now he turned and Flavia saw his face grow deep pink with rage.

'Domitian!' he gritted out from between clenched teeth. 'By the gods I'll ...' The ivory feet of his throne scraped on marble as he shoved it aside and hurried down his private stairs.

'Caesar!' Calvus called after him. 'You can't leave now! The children are saluting you! And you must inspect the weapons ...' his voice trailed off and he looked around the box sheepishly.

'I'll inspect the weapons,' announced Julia suddenly, and moved to sit in her father's throne.

Down in the arena, two slaves had pushed forward movable steps. The lanista mounted these steps so that his head and shoulders rose up on the other side of the parapet. Two guards clinked forward and stood protectively on either side of Julia, for the lanista held deadly weapons on a long wooden tray.

'What am I supposed to do?' Flavia heard Julia say.

'Just check them for sharpness,' replied the lanista, 'by lightly touching –'

'Ow!' squealed Julia and her hazel eyes widened in horror as she saw the blood oozing from a cut on her forefinger.

Sisyphus shrieked and Flavia cringed as both guards swung their swords out of their scabbards and pressed the points to the lanista's chest.

'Whoa!' The man tottered for a moment on the steps. 'I told her to touch it lightly!'

'My dear, are you hurt!' cried Sabinus, who had leapt to his feet.

'I did touch it lightly!' Julia ignored her husband and scowled at the lanista.

The guards withdrew their swords but left them unsheathed.

The lanista swallowed. 'Then you ... approve of the sharpness, domina?'

'Yes, yes.' Julia flapped her hand dismissively. 'Go away. Have your wretched fight.'

While the movable steps were being rolled away, Julia slumped back into her father's chair and sucked the tip of her wounded finger. Sabinus leaned over her and murmured soothing words.

A referee in a long tunic had used his staff to draw a large circle in the sand and now the first pair stepped forward: Mus, the tiny net-girl, and Vulpina the secutrix.

Flavia sat forward, interested despite herself.

Mus and Vulpina had taken up their positions at the centre of the large circle and now they faced each other across the referee's long stick. Mus had mousy brown hair screwed into a tight topknot. Vulpina wore the smooth helmet of the secutor with its tiny round eyeholes. Her reddish-brown hair curled out from beneath the shiny helmet's lower rim. The referee tapped his staff smartly on the sand and quickly jumped back. This was the signal for the bout to begin.

The water organ struck up a cheerful tune as the two girl gladiators circled each other.

Suddenly little Mus darted forward, swinging a net in her right hand and trying to keep Vulpina at bay with the trident in her left. The crowd cheered this first move of the bout. Flavia realised that although the trident was only half-sized, it was far too heavy for the little girl. The three points kept dipping. Once, they almost touched the sand.

Vulpina lunged forward and swung out with her sword. It almost struck the tiny gladiatrix and the crowd gasped.

Lupus tugged Flavia's blanket. She ignored him.

For a while the two girl gladiators circled each other. Occasionally one would make a feint but neither of them had drawn blood yet. The crowd was beginning to get bored and some in the higher levels were chanting, 'Strike her, strike her, strike her ...' The water organ played a suspenseful tune.

Flavia realised that Vulpina was tiring, her movements were slower. But Mus was tiring, too. Abruptly, the little girl tried to cast her net, but it became entangled on the prongs of her trident.

Lupus's fingers were digging into Flavia's arm.

'What?' said Flavia and tore her gaze away from the battling girls. Lupus was pointing urgently towards the other child gladiators, quietly waiting their turn to fight.

'What?'

Lupus pointed towards a pair of boys standing with their backs to the Imperial Box.

They held their helmets under their right arms and their shields in their left.

'The boy holding the yellow shield?' hissed Flavia.

Lupus shook his head.

'The one next to him? With the short hair?'

Lupus nodded vigorously then reached across her and

tapped Nubia.

'I can't really see him,' said Flavia. 'What about him?'

Again, Lupus pointed urgently at the pair.

Suddenly Nubia gasped. Lupus nodded wildly.

'What? What is it?' asked Flavia, almost angry.

'Behold!' said Nubia rising to her feet. 'It is Jonathan!'

SCROLL XXV

'Where?' gasped Flavia, and then, 'Jonathan? How can Jonathan be a gladiator?'

'Jonathan?' cried Sisyphus, almost choking on a mouthful of wine.

'Who's Jonathan?' Julia sat forward in her father's ivory chair.

'He's our friend,' said Flavia. 'But I don't think that's him ... If he would just turn so I could see his face ...'

'I think it is him,' said Nubia breathlessly and Lupus nodded vigorously.

Flavia squinted at the pair. 'No. That boy has short hair. And he's taller than Jonathan. And much slimmer. Remember how plump Jonathan got last month?'

Suddenly the crowd roared and Julia screamed.

Flavia and the others saw that little Mus was down on the sand, a jet of blood pulsing from a gash on her arm. They were close enough to see that she was crying.

The referee held his staff between the girls to mark a break in the combat, while a man in a blue tunic rushed forward. It must be the medicus, thought Flavia, for he was binding the little girl's wound. He whispered something to her and as he moved away the little girl raised her uninjured arm – the right one – with her forefinger extended.

'That means she wants to be spared,' Sisyphus told them. 'She's asking for mercy ... but where is Titus to grant it?'

All over the amphitheatre people were waving white handkerchiefs and giving the 'thumbs up' sign.

The herald stepped forward.

'The prize and penalty will be determined by Caesar!' He peered up into the box and then frowned at Julia's exaggerated shrug. 'At a time which is ... should prove ... convenient to him. Next combat will be between Prometheus the Thracian and Hostis the Murmillo.'

'Pollux!' cursed Flavia, looking back at the short-haired boy. 'He just put his helmet on.' She stood up. 'JONATHAN?' she yelled. 'Is that you?'

Everyone in the box turned to look at her but down on the sand the Thracian did not react. He had brought his left leg forward, his shield up and his head down. Flavia sat back weakly, feeling slightly sick.

'Classic Thracian attack position,' whispered Sisyphus. 'Whoever that boy is, he knows what he's doing.'

The water organ struck a chord a moment after the referee tapped the sand. The bout was on.

The two armed boys circled each other.

'He doesn't move like Jonathan,' observed Flavia after a while.

'That leg padding and those tall greaves would make anyone move stiffly,' said Sisyphus.

Lupus nodded his agreement.

'Helmets have bug eyes,' said Nubia. 'And feathers are like ...'

'Antennae,' murmured Flavia, without taking her eyes from the pair. 'Backwards antennae ...'

Suddenly Lupus grunted, urgently tapped his left shoulder, then pointed towards the boy gladiator.

'Yes!' cried Nubia. 'He has branding like Jonathan!'

'Is it a brand?' Flavia squinted. 'Or just a wound? What's he called again?'

Lupus had been studying his *libellus* – the gladiator form sheet – and now he excitedly pointed to a name on the sheet.

Under the heading NOVELTY GLADIATORS was a list of names. Flavia gasped when she saw the last name on the list.

It was Prometheus.

Prometheus.

Flavia sat back heavily and stared out at the fighting gladiators.

'*When Prometheus opens Pandora's box, Rome will be devastated ...*' she whispered to herself, and repeated what she had said at Jonathan's tomb: 'I should have known it would be about a fire.'

She thought back to the moment Lupus had brought Jonathan's charred rings. He had been accompanied by Titus's astrologer, Ascletario. The Egyptian had said – what were his words exactly? *There is a rumour that a boy set the fire at the Temple of Jupiter – a boy with dark curly hair and a bruised face.*

Flavia had assumed that Jonathan had tried to stop Prometheus, and died in the attempt. But if this boy gladiator was Jonathan, and if he called himself Prometheus ...

She shivered and stared straight ahead, searching for more clues in the past.

'Jonathan,' she whispered at last, 'was it *you*? Were you the one who started the fire?'

Nubia was tapping her arm. Flavia looked at her friend.

'When the Titus returns shall we tell him that one is maybe Jonathan?' Nubia asked.

'No! Whatever you do,' she hissed, 'don't tell Titus. If that boy is Jonathan, then I think ... I think he may have started the fire after all.'

Nubia, Lupus and Sisyphus all turned to stare at her.

'I'm not sure,' she said hastily. 'It might have been an accident and ... I don't know! We have to talk to him.'

'If he is still alive,' said Nubia, and pointed towards the arena.

Ira was trembling.

The instant after he put on his helmet he had heard someone shout out his old name.

The voice had sounded just like a friend's. Had his old life finally caught up with him? Or had he imagined it? Or was it some strange premonition of his death?

Until a moment ago he had been calm and prepared. Even for death.

But the girl's voice calling his name had brought back memories. A crowd of feelings and images which pushed against a door in his mind. He had to keep that mental door shut. He could not allow feelings in. Emotions made him weak.

All except for one. Anger.

Anger gave him strength. Anger loosened his chest and stopped him wheezing. He had chosen the name Ira, which meant anger, to complement his arena name. He needed that anger now.

And if he didn't find the anger soon, his opponent would win.

SCROLL XXVI

Ira the Thracian was finding it hard to breathe. All his carefully stored up anger had drained away with one word: his old name.

His opponent knocked him back with a heavy murmillo's shield and Ira only just managed to bring up his small parma in time to block a jabbing sword thrust. Hostis crashed into Ira again and he almost fell back onto the sand. Even through his padded helmet, he heard the crowd jeer.

Now that, THAT made him angry.

The tightness in his chest began to ease and the breath came. As Hostis charged again Ira darted the curved blade of his sica out from the protection of his shield. Hostis flinched as the sharp point bit into the soft skin beneath his left arm.

'*Habet!*' Ira heard the crowd roar even over the amplified sound of his own breathing.

His opponent retaliated by jabbing low with his sword, but the padding on Ira's upper leg protected him and he thrust again. Hostis swung his shield round to protect himself and sparks flew as Ira's curved sword glanced off the metal boss of the murmillo's big shield. Ira felt the vibration of metal on metal through his entire body.

Rotundus had warned them that in the heat of a

combat you sometimes didn't notice wounds. But Ira felt a searing pain as his opponent's sword sliced into the tender part of his left shoulder. *'Habet!'* came the cry of the crowd. The pain fuelled his anger.

Now the anger was building and Ira imagined Hostis was his great enemy, the man he hated most in the world. The Emperor Titus.

'What's happening?' said Titus, coming heavily up the stairs into the Imperial Box.

Lupus glanced round quickly then turned back to the fight.

'Caesar!' exclaimed Calvus, moving forward. 'You're just in time. The first combat is over and it looks as if the second is nearing its end, too. Quickly! Come sit!' Julia sighed and vacated her father's chair and as Titus resumed his throne Lupus heard Calvus say under his breath: 'Vulpina the secutrix bested Mus – the retiaria – but the little one fought bravely. The crowd wants her spared.'

'Of course we'll spare her,' said Titus from between gritted teeth. 'This is monstrous: having children fight. Monstrous. What's happening there?'

'Ah, Prometheus is the Thracian and the murmillo is Hostis. They've both been struck.'

Ira charged forward, uttering a bellow that resounded in the metal world of his helmet and deafened him for a moment. Hostis took a defensive position, his shield up, braced for the blow. But it never came. At the last moment Ira stopped, feinted right, then sidestepped left and brought the lower edge of his small shield down hard on the murmillo's right wrist.

Hostis cried out as the sword flew from his hand. Momentarily defenceless, Hostis tried to use his shield as a weapon. But it was big and heavy and as he jabbed its lower edge forward, Ira easily avoided it.

Failing to connect and momentarily off-balance, Hostis staggered.

In that instant, Ira swung his left leg round so that the heavy greave struck Hostis behind the knee. The murmillo's legs went and he was down.

Ira heard the crowd's cheer as he kicked his opponent's shield aside and pressed his foot hard on the boy's chest.

The referee's stick was there immediately but Ira was in control. He waited until the referee announced 'Prometheus has won the bout!'

Then Ira stepped back and removed his helmet with trembling hands.

Without his helmet on, the world seemed suddenly immense and bright and cool. He could hear the roaring of the crowd and he almost smiled. His anger was gone, replaced by relief. It was over. He had won.

The referee had removed Hostis's helmet, and Jonathan saw his mess-mate lying on the sand: no longer an opponent, but just a frightened boy.

Suddenly his relief faded and his stomach clutched.

What if the Emperor asked him to execute Hostis? Could he take his own friend's life?

Lupus had to use every iota of self-control not to shout with joy as the young Thracian removed his helmet.

It was Jonathan.

He was sure of it. He looked at his friends and saw his certainty reflected in their faces. Flavia and Nubia were hugging each other and Sisyphus was clapping loudly.

Almost immediately, Flavia put her forefinger to her lips and gave them a quick warning frown. As soon as they nodded, to show they had understood, Flavia's face relaxed into a delighted smile again.

But Lupus suddenly had a terrible thought. What if Titus recognised Jonathan? Even if Jonathan hadn't set the fire, the Emperor knew the rumour like everyone else. And if he put together the pieces ...

The Emperor had risen to his feet and was glaring down into the arena.

Lupus held his breath.

'Send them off!' Titus commanded.

'But Caesar!' said Calvus, 'you haven't awarded the palm branches or the crowns. And three of the pairs haven't fought yet!'

'Get them out of the arena!' repeated Titus from between clenched teeth. 'I refuse to take part in this travesty.'

As the child gladiators marched back out of the arena the crowd uttered mixed cries of protest and approval.

But Lupus sat back and breathed a huge sigh of relief.

The bright blast of trumpets and the surge of the water organ made Nubia's spirit soar. The sound perfectly expressed the joy in her heart.

Jonathan was alive. Alive!

She sat very still within herself, staring out at the vast arena, her vision blurred by tears of happiness. The child gladiators had left the arena – all of them fit enough to walk – and slaves had raked the sand clean.

Suddenly Nubia gasped as a rainbow shimmered in the vast space before her. A fine perfumed mist was being sprayed on the crowd from high above. Nubia inhaled, it was wonderful.

'Saffron,' whispered Flavia beside her and stretched her hand out from under the protection of the box so that she could feel it.

Abruptly a pink light covered her arms and tunic and those at the front of the Imperial Box. Nubia looked up. The red canvas vela were unfurling high above them.

'Ooh! Isn't it glorious!' Sisyphus perched beside her on the velvet-covered couch, a silver cup in his hand. 'Ruby light, exotic perfume, chilled wine ...' he lowered his voice to a whisper, 'and Jonathan resurrected! Life is good!'

A moment later, the arena was filled with shouts and shrieks as a swarm of red lottery balls scattered over the middle levels.

In that instant, Nubia knew what she could do. Her hand reached for her leather coin purse.

Was the lottery ball still there? Yes! With trembling fingers she undid the leather thong and pulled out the red ball.

'Oh!' gasped Julia. 'You won a lottery ball!'

'Nubia!' cried Sisyphus in an injured voice. 'Why didn't you tell me?'

'I forgot,' said Nubia, unscrewing the ball and taking out the square of parchment. 'Caesar, yesterday I have won a gladiator.'

'A gladiator?' Titus turned and raised his eyebrows in surprise.

'Yes, Caesar.'

Titus leaned over, stretched out his muscular arm and took the token. For a moment he examined it, both front and back.

Nubia took a deep breath. 'May I be taking any gladiator right now?' She could barely hear her own voice above the violent pounding of her heart.

'I don't see why not.' He gave Nubia an amused glance. 'Does one of them take your fancy?'

'Yes. I would like one to be free.'

'A strange request. Usually people rent them back to the lanista or employ them as bodyguards. You merely want to set one free?'

'Yes, Caesar. May I choose now?'

'I'm sorry?' said Titus. 'Could you –'

Nubia saw his lips moving but couldn't hear his words.

A roar so enormous it even drowned out the trumpets was sweeping the amphitheatre. The main event of the day was beginning.

The real gladiators were entering the arena.

There were about thirty of them, preceded by officials and musicians, and followed by slaves and attendants carrying their weapons. Last of all marched a man with a banner that read: LVDVS IVLIANVS.

'Nubia!' gasped Sisyphus, his dark eyes wide. 'It's the Ludus Julianus!'

Nubia looked blank.

Titus glanced over at them. 'The Ludus Julianus is the school founded by Julius Caesar, if I'm not mistaken.'

'That's right, Caesar,' said Sisyphus and looked

pointedly at Nubia. 'It's the gladiator school based in Capua!'

Nubia felt dizzy and her hand went automatically to her throat. Capua. The gladiators marching into the arena were from Capua. The place where her brother Taharqo was training to be a gladiator.

Nubia rose unsteadily to her feet and scanned the muscular men as they began their warm-up bout on the sand tinted pink by the awnings.

She saw him almost at once. Slim and muscular with a neat head and woolly black hair. And skin the same dark brown as hers.

'Behold,' whispered Nubia, and she didn't know whether to laugh or cry. 'It is my brother Taharqo.'

SCROLL XXVII

'Taharqo,' said Nubia, and her voice did not seem her own. 'It is Taharqo!'

'Who?' said Titus. 'Pantherus the Nubian?'

'It's Taharqo. Her brother!' gasped Flavia. 'I knew he'd be here!'

'Pantherus is your brother?' The Emperor turned to look at Nubia.

Nubia's throat was dry and she felt dizzy but she managed to nod.

'He's very handsome,' breathed Julia.

'A wonderful specimen,' agreed her husband.

'Bad news,' said Titus, looking at his programme. 'He's paired with Sextus.'

'*The* Sextus?' asked Julia's husband.

'I'm afraid so,' said Titus.

'Is that bad?' asked Flavia.

'Do you know why they call him Sextus?' asked Titus.

They all shook their heads.

'They call him Sextus because he's six feet tall and he has six fingers on each hand!'

Lupus consulted his *libellus* and looked up in alarm. He held up nine fingers.

'He has nine fingers on one hand?' asked Nubia.

'No.' Titus said grimly. 'He won each of his last nine bouts.'

151

'And now, for our last combat of the day,' announced the herald, 'Sextus the secutor, winner of nine palms and five wreathes, fights Pantherus the retiarius, a *tiro*, in his first combat!'

Lupus saw the referee raise his staff, then bring it down swiftly to strike the sand.

As the two began to circle one another, the crowd went silent and the water organ began to play. Lupus leaned forward and rested his forearms on the cool marble balustrade. The knowledge that Jonathan was alive had lifted an enormous weight from his spirit. He knew they would find some way to bring him home. Meanwhile, this was the perfect seat. He could see every detail of the fighting men. He would relax and enjoy this bout as he had enjoyed the others.

Both men were barefoot and Lupus felt a thrill of revulsion as he saw the secutor's six-toed foot shuffling forward in the sand. Sextus had padding on his right arm and left leg, and he wore the distinctive helmet of the secutor. Lupus had seen crude drawings of secutors scratched on walls but until today he had never seen one in real life. The strange smooth helmet with its tiny round eyeholes made the secutor look inhuman, more like a fish than a bug.

'The helmet is smooth so the net and trident will slip off.' Titus leaned forward and Lupus saw him glance at Nubia. 'But if the net-man can get the right angle and amount of force ... I have seen a trident punch right through such a helmet. But your brother is doing exactly what he should be in the early stages of the bout. He's holding the trident in his left arm, keeping the secutor at bay. If he's any good, he'll tire out his oppon-ent, then bring the net round in a sweeping motion – you can see the little lead weights – and entangle his opponent's feet. Then a swift tug and he brings his opponent down. By the gods, he's magnificent ...' murmured Titus, almost to himself.

Lupus nodded slowly. Taharqo was magnificent. He was lithe and muscular and his skin was oiled and pol-ished until it shone like mahogany. He wore a white loincloth and padding on his left arm. His belt and shoul-der-guard flashed in a bar of sunlight that had slipped through a gap in the vela. They looked like gold but Lupus guessed they were made of polished bronze. He knew gold was far too heavy and soft to serve as useful armour.

Taharqo was moving lightly on his feet and as the water organ and trumpets played dramatic music he improvised a little jig. The crowd laughed as Sextus stumped solidly forward, leading with his big, heavy shield.

Taharqo skipped behind him and Sextus had to swivel his whole body to find his opponent.

'I tried a secutor's helmet once,' said Sabinus from his seat beside Julia. 'The eyeholes are so small that you can only see straight ahead. And after a while your own breath begins to dry out your eyes. I hated wearing it.'

'Ha!' Titus pointed and laughed and sat back in his chair.

Taharqo had feinted right and then danced left, swing-ing the net around his head. The crowd was laughing and applauding. Taharqo was making it a comic routine, and the music was becoming less dramatic and more jaunty as the organist followed his lead.

Lupus could see the secutor's muscular chest rising and falling. The man was either angry or tiring. Or both. But he had won nine bouts against retiarii. Taharqo must not let his guard down.

Still dancing around Sextus, Taharqo switched his net to his left and his trident to the right. He was a safe distance away from the secutor, playing to the crowd. He placed the dull end of his trident in the sand and leaned on it like an old man, bending his back and slowly hobbling forward. The crowd laughed as the organist obliged by playing the tune usually reserved for the old father in the theatre.

But Lupus knew the crowd wouldn't be amused by Taharqo's antics for much longer. They wanted to see contact. They wanted to see blood. Lupus knew this because suddenly he wanted to see blood, too. He wanted to see it spurt in a joyful jet of red.

Taharqo must have sensed the crowd's mood, because at that moment he jabbed his trident out and then back, quick as a frog's tongue. At first Lupus thought he had missed. Then he saw the blood flowing from the thigh on Sextus's unprotected leg.

At the sight of first blood Lupus yelled. The crowd roared with him and the water organ sang out a triumphant chord.

Sextus turned heavily but Taharqo simply danced behind him, transferring the trident back to his left hand and the net to his right.

Suddenly – in one shockingly rapid movement – the secutor bent, turned, swung out his heavy shield in a smooth arc.

Taharqo raised his trident to parry, but the heavy shield slammed into it with such force that it broke the trident in half. The section with the prongs fell within the circle and rest of the shaft outside. The look of surprise had not fully formed on Taharqo's handsome face when Sextus lunged forward, and fast as a serpent's strike jabbed his short sword towards Taharqo's belly.

The crowd gasped and Taharqo leapt back but there was a clang of metal on metal.

The music surged dramatically.

Beside him, Titus was tutting and shaking his head. 'Pantherus was very lucky,' he said. 'His belt protected him. If that stroke had been an inch higher his entrails would be spilling onto the sand now.'

'And you could see the surprise on his face,' said Julia's husband. 'That's one of the easiest ways to tell a novice. Experienced gladiators never reveal their feelings.'

Another dramatic chord from the water organ and a sharp intake of breath from the whole amphitheatre. Sextus had made another lightning thrust with his short sword.

In a spray of his own blood, Taharqo was down on the sand.

SCROLL XXVIII

Nubia didn't want to look at the blood flowing from her brother's side but she couldn't turn away. This was her own brother. She couldn't hide her face in her hands this time.

'Don't worry,' Flavia said beside her. 'I think it's just a flesh wound.'

'It's not too grave,' agreed Titus, without taking his eyes from the arena.

Now the music was low, soft, urgent. Taharqo was up, wary now, no longer clowning for the crowd. He still had his net and dagger, and had recovered the top half of his trident. But none of these offered proper defence.

He and Sextus circled one another. Both had drawn blood, both were sweating, both tired. Outside the ring the referee circled, too, every bit as focused as the men within the ring.

Then Taharqo made his move. He flicked out his right hand and the net flowed over the sand in a smooth, low curve. Sextus staggered back. But Taharqo had taken another step forward and now the net flowed from left to right. Nubia saw the tiny lead weights flick it round both Sextus's ankles.

Taharqo gave a swift tug and Sextus fell back, landing hard on the sand. Nubia heard his grunt even above the roar of the crowd.

'Perfect!' cried Titus and brought his fist lightly down on the marble balustrade.

Taharqo had already let go of his net and had run forward to stamp on Sextus's sword arm with his bare foot. The sword fell onto the sand.

'Kick it away!' cried Titus.

But Taharqo did not take the Emperor's advice. Slipping his own dagger into his belt he bent to grasp the secutor's sword. Just as he did so, Sextus brought his left arm round and slammed his shield into Taharqo, who fell with such violence that the sword flew right out of his hand, right out of the circle.

The people cheered, and Titus turned, his face alive. 'The sword fell outside the circle, so it's out of play.'

Now Sextus was up and Taharqo was down, but the net was still around the secutor's feet. As Sextus raised his heavy shield in order to slam the edge onto his opponent's neck, Taharqo grasped a corner of the net.

He tugged.

Down came Sextus. Up jumped Taharqo. This time the Nubian grabbed the shield and twisted it. Even over the roar of the crowds and the urgent water organ Nubia heard a sickening crack. The secutor's arm was broken and his heavy shield was no longer a defence but an agonising burden.

The amphitheatre erupted into cheers loud enough to drown out the triumphant music as Taharqo retrieved his broken trident and strutted around Sextus, smiling up at the crowds with his dazzling white teeth.

'Pantherus! Pantherus!' the crowd was chanting.

'Don't get cocky, my dear boy,' Nubia heard Sisyphus say. 'It's not over yet.'

At that very instant, Sextus twisted his body to one side and reached out his terrible six-fingered right hand to grasp Taharqo's ankle and bring him down. But Taharqo must have been waiting for this. Quick as lightning his left hand brought down the trident, pinning the secutor's wrist to the sand.

Blood spurted and even from under the tight smooth helmet Nubia could hear the secutor's bellow of pain. The terrible cry was cut off as Taharqo placed his dark foot on the big man's pale neck.

'*Habet, habet!*' cried the crowds. 'He's had it!'

Now the head referee stepped forward. He touched Taharqo's foot lightly with his staff and said something under his breath. Taharqo nodded and Nubia saw him ease his foot a fraction from the secutor's neck.

'I declare Pantherus the victor!' cried the referee, 'winner of the palm of victory ...' Here the referee looked at Titus, who nodded. 'And of the wreath!'

'I declare Sextus the loser,' continued the referee. 'Does he deserve death or a *missio*?'

Nubia saw Titus rise to his feet. He looked at the senators around him and the Vestals opposite him and the crowds above him. A few people were waving handkerchiefs but most had turned their thumbs down and were calling out: '*Iugula*! Stab him in the throat!'

Titus turned and looked at Calvus.

She couldn't hear him clearly, but she thought the Emperor said, 'Sextus fought well. Must I do as the crowd requests?'

Calvus nodded and said something with an apologetic look.

Nubia saw the Emperor's shoulders rise and fall in a

deep sigh. But he stretched out his hand and slowly turned his thumb to the ground.

There was a thunderous cheer which quickly died to a smattering of applause.

And now the amphitheatre grew quiet as the people held their breath. This was a sacred moment. The victorious Nubian must cut the throat of his own companion, a man he had trained with, eaten with, laughed with. A man from his own *familia*.

The lanista moved forward and gently removed the secutor's tight helmet. Then he said a few words to Sextus, who nodded. Nubia knew that although the secutor's arm was broken and he was bleeding from three places, none of the wounds were fatal. He must nevertheless offer his throat bravely.

The lanista tossed aside Sextus's shield and helped him kneel on the sand. Then he handed Taharqo a short sword and stepped back. The final act must be between victor and vanquished.

'This is what we Romans come to see,' murmured Titus in a voice so low Nubia could barely hear him, 'the example of how a brave man dies.'

There was no way Sextus could have heard him, but at that moment he slowly lifted his head and looked up at the Emperor. Titus smiled at him and gave a nod so small that Nubia would never have seen it from the highest tier.

The beaten gladiator turned from the Emperor to Taharqo and Nubia saw no fear in his eyes before he closed them. Swiftly and without hesitation, Taharqo plunged the gladius through the base of Sextus's throat towards his heart. A fountain of blood sprayed Taharqo and Nubia put her hot face in her cold hands.

But the crowd's cheering and jaunty water organ went on for so long that presently she looked up again.

Her brother and the other winning gladiators were jogging their lap of honour round the arena. Like the others, Taharqo brandished the palm branch in his right hand and a money-pouch in the other. And like the others he wore a look of elated triumph on his face

'So, Nubia,' said the Emperor Titus, leaning back in his ivory chair with a wide smile. 'I take it Pantherus is the gladiator you would like me to set free? What a shame for the rest of us. He shows great promise.'

Nubia stared at Titus. 'Yes. No. I don't know,' she whispered.

'What?' said Titus, his smile fading and his eyebrows going up. 'But I thought all this was about your brother. Surely he's the one you had in mind when you asked me if you could free any gladiator?'

'I ... I don't know, Caesar.' stammered Nubia. She felt like crying. She couldn't set them both free. Only one. Either Taharqo or Jonathan. Her brother or her friend.

'Well, you don't have to make your decision immediately. Why don't you go over to the Oppian Hill after the games and have a closer look at them.'

'I ... will they... I ...'

'Say yes!' hissed Flavia. 'Then at least we can talk to them.'

'Yes,' said Nubia. 'Thank you, Caesar. Thank you.'

Titus glanced at one of his guards and the man nodded.

'Fronto will take you to see the gladiators this evening,

if you like,' said Titus, rising to his feet. 'Then you can tell me in the morning. I hope you and your friends will join us tomorrow as well. I'd like to know the outcome of this little drama!'

SCROLL XXIX

'Nubia, what a terrible dilemma!' Flavia shivered.

'What is die lemon?' asked Nubia, raising her head from her hands.

'A dilemma is a hard choice,' said Sisyphus.

The games were over for the day and the happily chattering crowds were pouring out of the amphitheatre. Titus and his entourage had left by the private entrance a moment earlier. The three friends and Sisyphus lingered in the Imperial Box, trying to decide what to do.

'You can set Jonathan free,' said Flavia, 'or you can set your brother free. But you can't do both. You have to choose.' She suddenly felt exhausted, and she noticed that Nubia looked as sick as she felt.

'I know,' whispered Nubia. 'And I do not know whom I should be choosing.'

Lupus had been writing on his wax tablet:

JONATHAN

'Of course you and I want it to be Jonathan,' Flavia said to him, pulling the blue blanket round her shoulders. 'But it's Nubia's brother. And her lottery ball. So it's Nubia's choice.'

Lupus turned away angrily. Flavia was wondering

how to comfort him when the cloying scent of honeysuckle from the garlands above sent a wave of nausea
over her.

'Flavia, my dear,' cried Sisyphus. 'Are you all right?'

Flavia nodded. Then shook her head. She felt hot. So
hot that she was sweating. She shrugged off the soft blue
blanket and rested her head in her hands.

The sound of jingling footsteps. A soldier's hobnailed
boots and muscular calves moved into her line of sight,
framed against the coloured diamonds of the inlaid
marble floor. Flavia lifted her head to see the big broken-
nosed soldier standing before their couch.

'My name is Fronto.' He was speaking to Nubia. 'I'm
to take you wherever you want to go.'

'I ... I want to see Jonathan and my brother,' said Nubia
looking at Flavia.

'The child gladiators,' said Flavia to the guard, 'and the
gladiators from Ludus Julianus.' She stood up. And then
sat heavily as her knees gave way beneath her.

She felt Sisyphus's cool hand on her forehead. 'Flavia!
You're burning up! I've got to get you home.'

'No, Sisyphus, we have to go with Nubia and Lupus.
We have to see Jonathan.' Suddenly she felt cold. The
honeyed scent of the flowers filled her throat again. She
put her head between her knees and took some deep
breaths.

Sisyphus said, 'Will you see them back to the Caelian
Hill after you've taken them to the gladiators?'

'What?' Flavia looked up and saw that he was addressing Fronto.

'Of course,' said the guard. Despite his broken nose he
had a big, pleasant face. 'I'll bring them safely back to

you.'

'Fine,' said Sisyphus. 'We live on the Caelian Hill at the foot of the aqueduct. Senator Cornix's house. Sky-blue door. Bronze knocker.'

'Aren't you coming with us?' Flavia asked Sisyphus. He seemed curiously remote.

Sisyphus ignored her.

'And if you please,' he said, 'will you find a litter so I can get this sick girl home?'

'But I have to go and see Jonathan,' murmured Flavia, stretching out on the imperial couch. 'I only need a little rest first.'

'We were here!' Nubia stopped, and looked around in wonder. 'Last year we were throwing trigon ball.'

The mellow light of late afternoon flooded the slope of the Oppian Hill.

Lupus nodded his agreement.

Without breaking his stride Fronto said over his shoulder, 'We're going to the Golden House. That's where the new School of Gladiators is located.'

'The Golden House!' exclaimed Nubia. 'But what about the women of Jerusalem? The ones who weave carpets?'

Fronto shrugged. 'They all moved out after the fire last month. Had to make way for the gladiators.'

He led them through a gate in the wall that Nubia did not remember and towards a stepped pathway that she did.

'Remember we were littered up this hill,' Nubia whispered to Lupus.

He nodded and pointed towards a peacock wandering

among the pink- and red-blooming rhododendron bushes.

As they topped the last few steps, the Golden House came into view. A long row of gilded columns blazed in the late sunshine and the reflecting pools seemed filled with molten gold. To the right, Nubia saw that dozens of pavilions had been erected on the green grass. Slaves were fixing torches in the ground, ready to be lit at dusk. A banner straight ahead read LVDVS AVREVS and one further away LVDVS IVLIANVS. She also saw signs that read LVDVS GALLICVS and LVDVS DACICVS.

Fronto led them straight on, between two reflecting pools. Nubia saw that these were no longer occupied by flamingos and herons, and the water lilies had been removed. As they passed between the golden pillars of the colonnade they came into a large courtyard. Nubia remembered running across it in pursuit of an assassin half a year before. Then it had been grassy. Now it was covered with sand.

A few men were sparring on the sand and one man was repeatedly striking a wooden post with his sword.

'Most of them will be at dinner,' said their guide. 'This way.'

Fronto led them into a high barrel-vaulted room off the exercise area. It was dim in here but torches burned in wall-brackets and Nubia immediately saw three long tables. The gladiators sat eating from red clay bowls.

Lupus pointed and Nubia cried, 'There he is!'

The boy whose arena name was Prometheus sat near the end of one table, hunched over his bowl, not talking to any of the men around him.

'Jonathan!' Nubia and ran towards him. 'Jonathan, you are alive!'

The boy slowly looked up.

Nubia had intended to hug him, but his cold expression stopped her short. 'Jonathan? What is wrong?'

'You've made a mistake,' he said. 'My name isn't Jonathan. It's Ira.'

Nubia glanced uncertainly at Lupus. He looked as stunned as she felt. Nubia wished Flavia were here. She would know what to say and do.

Everyone at the tables had stopped eating and Nubia felt all their eyes upon her.

'What's going on here?' A dark, stocky man came into the dining room. 'Ira, you know I don't allow –,' His eyes opened wide as Titus's soldier clinked forward. 'Fronto! What's wrong?'

Fronto stepped over to the shorter man and growled something in his ear.

'Oh, all right, then. Carry on,' he said to Fronto. Then he turned to Nubia. 'I'm Rotundus, the lanista here. Just ask me if you want any information.'

'I would like to talk to that one,' said Nubia politely in a voice which did not seem to be her own.

'Go ahead.'

'May I speak of privately?'

He nodded. 'Take them to your room, Ira.'

The boy's chair scraped on the concrete floor as he stood.

'Come on then.' His tone was curt and he did not look back at them as he walked out of the high vaulted room.

SCROLL XXX

Nubia and Lupus followed Ira out of the refectory and across the practice area. The sun had dropped behind some trees and cast long blue shadows on the sloping lawn. The sand slipping between Nubia's sandalled toes was cool and soft. A man hitting the post stopped to stare at them as they passed.

'Give the poor palus a break, Attius,' said Ira without looking at him.

Attius laughed and resumed his practice.

Nubia watched Ira. He seemed completely at home in this strange world of men and weapons. He was like Jonathan. And yet he was not like Jonathan.

They followed him into another vaulted room. Its walls and ceiling were lavishly decorated with frescoes in blue, black, yellow and cinnabar red. But the furnishings were spartan: eight simple cots with small tables at their heads and chests at their feet.

Ira sat on a cot and gestured for the others to do the same. Nubia sat on the cot next to him but Lupus remained standing.

'Why are you here?' said Ira, in a flat voice.

Nubia glanced at Lupus and swallowed.

'We think you are dead,' she whispered. 'And we miss you very much. Especially Tigris. So when Rumour whispers that you might be alive we all come to find you.

Jonathan –'

'Don't call me that,' he said. 'My name is Ira. Jonathan is dead.'

Nubia stared at him. Had they all made a terrible mistake? Was this boy not Jonathan?

'Ira,' she said hesitantly. 'Today Flavia is nearly devoured by hippos, crocodiles and bears, Lupus turns informer, and I swoop down from the very top. So please be telling us how Jonathan died!'

He lifted his eyebrows in surprise, and this time Nubia saw a brief flicker of amusement in his eyes. Now she knew he was Jonathan.

He must have seen the certainty in her face because he dropped his head.

'Jonathan threw himself off the Tarpeian Rock. Or maybe he died of an asthma attack while training to be a gladiator. I don't know. But he's dead.'

There was a pause. Nubia glanced at Lupus, who was looking at Jonathan with huge wounded eyes.

'Jona – ... Ira,' said Nubia gently. 'We know what you are doing last month. It was accident, wasn't it?'

His head jerked up and Nubia saw that her words had broken some barrier. Hope gleamed in his eyes.

'Jonathan,' Nubia persisted, 'it doesn't matter if you set the fire. Don't you want to be free? Don't you want to go home?'

It seemed to Nubia that as she pronounced that last word, the hope in his eyes died like an ember in the snow.

He stood and looked down at her. 'I told you,' he said – and his voice had become cold again, 'Jonathan is dead. Now go away.'

*

Nubia felt numb as she and Lupus followed Fronto along the colonnade of the Golden House. To her right, beyond the dark looming bulk of the amphitheatre, the angry red sun seemed to be shrinking rather than setting, as if its blood was draining into the horizon.

Presently ropes blocked their way and they saw that couches had been laid out between the gilded columns and the reflecting pools up ahead.

Dozens of muscular men reclined on these couches. They all wore short cream tunics with a dark vertical stripe from each shoulder to hem. All were bathed and perfumed and their muscular oiled bodies gleamed like ivory, oak, mahogany, and ebony. Long-haired slave-boys attended them and behind the barrier of the pools dozens of men and women stood gazing at them.

The gladiators were eating, but they might have been on stage. The torches were being lit and off to one side musicians banged tambourines and blew buzzy double reeds.

As they walked past the audience on the other side of the reflecting pools, Nubia saw that most of the observers were rich and highborn. One man, a grey-haired senator, had bent over and was murmuring in his son's ear, pointing first at one gladiator, then at another. It seemed to Nubia that there were many more women than men. Most wore their pallas pulled up over their elaborate hairdos.

'Do these people also have gladiator balls?' Nubia asked Fronto.

Fronto looked startled. Then he laughed. 'No. But like you, they have an interest in gladiators. Some are buyers.

Some want a close look at who they're betting on. Most of the ladies just like to look, though one or two might go to a gladiator's tent.' His smile faded and he spat. 'That's why these women hide their faces with their cloaks. They are supposed to be *respectable*. A few are even married.'

'There is Taharqo.' Nubia's heart was pounding. 'May I speak to him?'

Fronto shook his head. 'Afraid not. That's not the way it's done. You'll have to stand opposite him and catch his eye. After he's eaten, he'll come to you. If he's interested.'

Lupus pointed at the group of women waiting opposite Taharqo's couch and he raised his eyebrows.

'Yes,' said Fronto. 'Pantherus is very popular with the girls. Looks like you'll have to wait your turn, young lady.'

But Nubia didn't have to wait at all.

As soon as Taharqo caught sight of her, his face broadened into a smile, he slipped off his couch and splashed through the reflecting pool towards her.

'Little sister!' he said in their language. 'I thought I saw you today sitting in the Emperor's Box. And now look, here you are!' He hugged her and even through his soft tunic and bandaged chest she could feel his heart beating. Nubia held him tightly. It was really him. Her beloved oldest brother. Alive.

There were so many things she wanted to say to him. So many questions. So many laments. So many recollections. The emotions seemed to rise up in her like a wine poured into a too-small jug and they spilled over as hot tears.

'I know,' he murmured. 'It was a terrible thing. Terrible.'

For a long time Nubia's brother held her, until her tears finally subsided.

Then he held her out at arm's length and smiled down at her. Nubia was suddenly aware of all the people around them: Lupus, Fronto and half a dozen curious women, staring at them and watching them in the twilight.

Lupus held out his grubby handkerchief. Nubia took it and blew her nose and smiled at Taharqo.

'This is my friend Lupus,' said Nubia in Latin.

'I am honoured to meet you,' replied her brother in good Latin. Then he looked at a pretty young woman standing beside Lupus. 'And who are you?' he asked.

'Oooh!' The girl gave a gasp of excitement and took a step closer. 'My name is Chriseis and I think you're wonderful!' Nubia saw that she had lovely green eyes, creamy skin, and a curvy figure.

Taharqo winked at Chriseis. 'Don't go anywhere,' he said in Latin and turned back to Nubia.

'My next combat is in three days,' he said in their own language, catching her cold hands in his warm ones. 'Will you come again?'

'Taharqo,' said Nubia. 'I have a gladiator ball. You can be free.'

'You what?' he dropped her hands as Nubia fished in her coin pouch.

His eyes opened wide. 'Oh! A lottery ball! You won a lottery ball?'

Nubia nodded and tears of joy welled up in her eyes.

'And the gods granted that I could choose a gladiator. I can choose you, Taharqo. You can come home with me to Ostia. You can be free.'

Taharqo threw back his head and laughed. 'Free?' he said. 'Free?'

He stepped forward, caught Chriseis round the waist and pulled her close. The girl squealed and gazed up at him in naked adoration.

'Free of pretty girls like this one?' continued Taharqo in their own language. 'Free of the best food I've ever eaten? Free of a bedroom with painted walls, a pouch of gold after every game and my own private slave to massage me? Free of the adulation of the Roman people? Dearest little sister, why would I want to be free?'

'Don't cry, Nubia,' said Flavia from her bed. 'Or you'll get me started again.'

Nubia and Lupus were back at Senator Cornix's household, sitting on chairs in the girls' lamplit bedroom. Flavia was tucked up in bed with Tigris. It was dark outside, but Sisyphus had tried to brighten the room with so many lamps that the sweet smell of olive oil filled the room. He had just brought in another.

'Look,' said Flavia. 'Here's Niobe with your dinner. You'll feel better when you've eaten something.'

Senator Cornix's cook – a silent slave-woman – handed Lupus a beaker of fermented milk and placed a tray of cold meats and salad on Nubia's lap.

'Poor Nubia,' said Sisyphus, perching on Flavia's bed. 'Your lottery ball might have bought the freedom of two people dear to you. But neither of them wanted it. How ironic.'

'I think I can understand why Taharqo refused,' said Flavia, stroking Tigris's head thoughtfully. 'What would he do if he wasn't a gladiator?'

Sisyphus nodded sadly. 'And the life of a gladiator can be very seductive.'

Flavia leaned back against her pillows and stared up at the flickering ceiling. 'But why doesn't Jonathan want to be free?'

Nobody answered so she answered her own question.

'I'm certain now,' she said slowly, 'that Jonathan did start the fire.'

Lupus put down his beaker and gave her his bug-eyed look.

'It's the only explanation,' said Flavia, sitting forward. 'It fits all the clues. The rumour that a boy with curly hair started the fire. The fact that Jonathan is so hard, and calls himself Ira. That he chose Prometheus for his arena name. Think about it. The fire killed thousands of people. I think if I'd done something so terrible I'd want to change my name and forget my past.'

'But why?' asked Nubia, and Flavia noticed she had hardly touched her food. 'Why would Jonathan do such a terrible thing as set the fire?'

'Remember the last thing that happened before Jonathan ran away?' said Flavia. 'The Emperor professed undying love to Jonathan's mother and then yelled at Jonathan to get out?'

They all nodded.

'Jonathan must have been so angry at Titus – and so hurt about his mother – that he went up to the temple on the Capitoline Hill and set the fire.'

'Maybe,' said Nubia slowly, 'Jonathan is not even

knowing his mother is home in Ostia. Maybe he thinks she is still living in palace with the Titus.'

'Great Neptune's beard, Nubia!' cried Flavia. 'You're right! The last thing Jonathan saw was Titus knock his father to the ground and tell his mother he loved her. He might not even know his parents are together again.'

'Maybe if we tell him, he would want to be Jonathan again.'

'Or maybe not,' murmured Flavia and gazed sadly down at Tigris. 'If you had killed thousands of people, would you want your parents to know?'

Nubia looked at Tigris's hopefully panting face and began to weep again.

'You three,' said Sisyphus gently, 'have had quite a day. I know I have. It is an hour past sunset and long past your bedtime. I advise you to go to bed and get a good night's sleep. As for you, young lady,' he said to Flavia. 'I'm giving you the last of Senator Cornix's sleeping potion. You need to spend the night sleeping, not worrying.'

Jonathan woke up sweating. He had been having the fire dream again and his heart was thumping.

The film of sweat on his skin had turned cold and he shivered and pulled his thin blanket round him like a cloak. Then he got up from his cot and went out of the vaulted room to breathe the night air. A wall-torch flickered somewhere behind him and threw his strange faint shadow far ahead of him.

How had he come to be back here at the Golden House, where half a year ago he had first discovered his mother was alive?

Was he dreaming?

Was he dead?

The full moon's silvery light made the frescoed designs on the high walls look black and grey. Like Nubia's Land of Grey. Like the underworld.

If only he could turn back the hours and undo what he had done. If only he could go to the underworld and bring back his mother. If only he could die to save her.

He stepped out into the sandy practice area and looked up at the full moon, rising silver to her zenith. There was something about that moon. Something special. It nagged at the back of his memory but he couldn't find the answer.

He heard a soft chanting. A phrase, a response, coming from somewhere to his left. Frowning, he moved silently back into a high corridor and saw the flickering bar of light beneath a door.

He stood outside, holding his breath and listening. From inside a man's voice repeating a phrase his father often recited: 'This is my blood, shed for the forgiveness of sins. Whenever you drink it, think of me.'

Then he remembered. It was not merely the moon that was special. This night was special, too. It was Passover.

Jonathan pushed open the door and entered.

Three startled faces turned towards Jonathan. One was Exactor, a bankrupt tax-collector who had sold himself to the school and fought as a Thracian. The other two were ex-slaves. One was a hoplomachus called Alexamenos and the third man was a Judaean who also fought as a Thracian. Jonathan couldn't remember his name.

'Ira,' said Exactor with a guilty look. 'What are you –?

It was a small room – one of the smallest in the Golden House – and the three men sat cross-legged on the floor by a table. The only objects on the table were half a bread roll and a ceramic cup of wine, which gleamed ruby red in the lamplight.

'The Lord's supper,' whispered Jonathan and looked at them in amazement. 'You're Christians.'

Alexamenos smiled at Jonathan and nodded. 'Would you like to join us, Ira? Are you a believer?'

Jonathan paused and thought.

'No,' he said at last. 'Not any more.'

Then he slowly turned and walked out of the room.

Nubia slipped into the deep, dreamless sleep of emotional exhaustion. Near dawn she rose out of this welcome oblivion to somewhere near consciousness.

She knew she was dreaming when she saw Jonathan on top of a sun-bleached hill. But she couldn't stop the dream from playing out before her. Apart from Jonathan, there was nothing on the hill but thorns and thistles and a large flat stone. Suddenly a man in long black robes appeared. He had ropes in his hands. The man said something to Jonathan, who nodded and lay on the hot stone. The man bent over him and bound his feet and wrists.

In Nubia's dream, the man gently pushed Jonathan's head back to expose the vulnerable throat. Then the man took something from his black robes and as he lifted his hand Nubia saw the flash of a blade.

Just as the man brought his knife down, Nubia woke up.

PROGRAMME OF EVENTS

INAUGURAL GAMES DAY III
TO BE HELD AT THE NEW AMPHITHEATRE

ETRUSCAN DANCERS
A HUNT OF HOUNDS AND EXOTIC BEASTS
EXECUTION OF A CRIMINAL
in which an arsonist will die
reenacting the torment of Prometheus

COMBAT OF NOVELTY GLADIATOR PAIRS
featuring dwarves and cripples

COMBAT OF GLADIATORS

AWNINGS AND DRINKS WILL BE PROVIDED

PRIZES WILL BE DISTRIBUTED

SCROLL XXXI

The Emperor Titus turned to Nubia.

'Where is Flavia Gemina?' he asked. 'And your guardian ... Tantalus, was it?'

It was a bright fresh morning on the third day of the inaugural games. Nubia and Lupus had just taken their seats on one of the upholstered couches in the Emperor's Box.

'Flavia is not well,' said Nubia. 'She is still sleeping fastly. Sisyphus stays with her to watch over her.'

'Poor girl,' said Titus. 'I hope she's recovered by this afternoon. We're going to make Fabius fight as an and-abata. Armour and a sharp sword but a helmet with no eyeholes. He and his opponents slash blindly at each other. I thought that would amuse her.'

Nubia stared at his cheerful face in horror.

His smile faltered. 'So, Nubia, have you decided which gladiator you would like?'

Nubia nodded.

She was just fishing her lottery ball out of her belt pouch when Fronto appeared at the top of the stairs and clanked to attention.

'The men you asked for, Caesar,' he said. 'They are here as you requested.'

'Show them in,' said Titus.

Fronto stood aside, and as two men come forward,

Lupus leapt to his feet in alarm.

'Africanus. Stertinius. Come. Sit.' Titus gestured towards an empty couch on the other side of his throne. 'I want everyone to see that I have pardoned you for conspiring against me.'

It was Lupus's turn to stare at the Emperor in horror.

'I am pontifex maximus now,' said Titus in Lupus's direction, loud enough so that the senators in the seats around could hear, 'and I intend to show great mercy while I hold that office.' He smiled at the men. 'Please sit and take some refreshment. And I hope you will dine with me this evening at the Palatine, as well. By the way, Africanus, I've sent word to your mother in Neapolis that you are well and safe.'

'Caesar!' Africanus fell to his knees and pressed his lips fervently to Titus's hand. 'You are merciful. Forgive us.'

'I already have.' Titus turned to Nubia. 'So, my dear,' he said. 'Who is it to be? Which gladiator would you like to take home?'

Nubia held out the wooden ball. 'Prometheus,' she said quietly. 'I would like to take Prometheus home.'

Titus raised his eyebrows. 'The boy gladiator from yesterday? The Thracian? He fought well ... but why not your own brother?'

'Because "Prometheus" is their friend,' said a female voice, 'their friend Jonathan.'

They all turned towards Julia, who was using a silver knife to cut slices of melon.

'What?' She looked at them, a cube of green melon poised on the tip of her knife. 'Isn't that what you said yesterday?'

Titus stared at his daughter, then slowly turned to Nubia.

'Your friend Jonathan?' he said. 'The boy gladiator who calls himself Prometheus is your friend Jonathan ben Mordecai? Susannah's son?'

Nubia looked at Lupus, then back at Titus, who had just shown mercy to men who had tried to murder him. Surely he would show mercy to Jonathan, too.

'Yes,' said Nubia bravely. 'Jonathan is alive.'

But the instant she said it, Nubia remembered the identity of the black-robed figure from her dream. She had thought it was Mordecai, but she now realised that the figure had been shorter, and stockier.

Titus rose to his feet. His face was very pale. '"When a Prometheus opens a Pandora's Box ...' he murmured and then he turned his head and said in a hard voice: 'Guards! Arrest the boy gladiator called Prometheus. And bring him here immediately.'

Nubia buried her face in her hands.

The realisation had come too late.

In her dream, the figure with the knife had been Titus.

When they brought Jonathan in to the Emperor's Box, Lupus stood up, struck again at the physical change in his friend. Jonathan's shaven head and muscular body made him look like a young thug. His shins were battered and the knuckles on both hands were skinned and swollen. And there was a new scar on his chin.

Jonathan glanced at Lupus, and then coldly looked away.

Lupus felt something like a blow to his heart and he sat on the couch again.

'Jonathan ben Mordecai,' said Titus. He pushed himself up from his throne and went to Jonathan.

Jonathan was almost as tall as the Emperor and the two of them stared into each other's eyes for a moment. Lupus saw Jonathan look away first.

'Tell me, Jonathan – and consider before you reply – it is widely reported that a boy with dark curly hair was seen on the Capitoline Hill the night the fire started. I believe we are holding a boy of that description down in the cells. He is due to be executed at noon today. Have we got the right boy? Or are you the one who started the fire?'

Jonathan did not reply.

'Does that boy deserve to die?'

'No,' said Jonathan at last, and added in a flat voice: 'It was an accident. I was trying to stop your enemy from –'

'Did you start the fire? Yes or no.'

'Yes, Caesar. I started the fire.'

'I thought as much.'

He turned to Fronto. 'Release the other boy and execute this one instead.' And to Jonathan. 'I'm sorry, Jonathan ben Mordecai, but in this case justice must be done.'

In the Imperial Box, Nubia knelt before Rome's first citizen and pressed her lips to his soft, freckled hand.

'Please, Caesar,' she begged. 'Please pardon Jonathan. It was being an accident.'

'Try to understand,' said Titus gently removing his hand and lifting her to the couch. 'I can pardon these two men who wanted me dead. That threat was to me personally and I must show the Roman people that I am not a second Nero. But the fire last month claimed thousands of lives. The Roman people demand vengeance. Someone must be seen to be responsible and pay for it. Do you understand?'

Nubia shook her head.

'Nubia. Lupus. Do you know what a scapegoat is? Jonathan's mother first told me. She told me that the sins of a community are transferred to a scapegoat and then that creature is killed. When the scapegoat is dead, the people are absolved.'

Lupus wrote on his tablet and held it up.

LIKE NERO BLAMED THE FIRE ON CHRISTIANS?

'I suppose,' said Titus with a frown. 'But isn't it better that one person dies rather than a whole community? And Jonathan is guilty in this matter. Even he admits that.'

'Jonathan is always believing things are his fault,' said Nubia quietly.

Titus passed his hand across his face. 'Jonathan committed one of the most terrible crimes there is, Nubia. And I promised the Roman people that I would punish the guilty. I can change the rules in the case of two battling gladiators, but in a matter like this ... How can I go against my own promise? Do you know how hard this is for me? To condemn the only son of someone I ... who means so much to me?'

'But Jonathan was dead,' said Nubia, tears pouring down her face, 'and now he is alive. How can you kill him again?'

Jonathan hardly noticed where they were taking him.

He felt a strange sense of relief. At least death would end his misery and his guilt. For not only had he killed thousands of Romans in the fire, but he bore the guilt of his mother's death.

He had given her a potion to make her sleep. Instead it had killed her.

He had wanted to die, too, but had convinced himself that he deserved to suffer. That was why he had given up his freedom to become a gladiator.

And so now, as they prodded him down the dark corridors below the amphitheatre and the guards spat on him, he did not flinch.

He deserved it.

When the other prisoners cursed him, he kept his face blank.

He deserved it.

But when the man with the wart on his eyelid smeared warm blood on Jonathan – to encourage the animal to attack him – Jonathan bent over and was sick on the straw covered floor.

He couldn't help it.

SCROLL XXXII

'Tigris! What is it?' murmured Flavia sleepily. 'Stop barking in my ear. TIGRIS!'

She sat up in bed. 'You're barking! Is Jonathan here? Did Nubia buy him with her lottery ball? Oh, Tigris, my mouth feels like the Cloaca Maxima.'

Flavia groped for the copper beaker on her bedside table and took a long drink of cold water.

'Look how high the sun is! It must be almost noon. Why didn't anyone wake me? Where's Sisyphus? Tigris! Stop barking!'

Flavia swung her feet out of bed and her toes groped for her sandals on the rough mosaic floor. Somewhere near the front of the house she heard the door-knocker banging. Tigris heard it, too, and was out of the bedroom like an arrow from a bow.

'Tigris! Come back! Where are you going? Tigris wait for me!'

'Death either destroys us or frees us.'

It had been a saying of Seneca's which Rotundus was fond of quoting. Sometimes when they ate dinner, the lanista would walk up and down behind them and quote the great Stoic philosopher:

'Always be prepared. Know that death is only a heart-beat away. To die honourably and splendidly; that is rare.

If you fear death, you will never do anything of greatness.' Then Rotundus would add: 'When the time comes for you to die, face it bravely. Honour this *familia* by your death.'

Now, as the cell door opened and the two soldiers stepped forward, Jonathan silently vowed. 'I will die a good death. One that will make my *familia* proud. And my friends, if they are watching.'

He tried not to let his knees tremble as the soldiers flanked him and gripped his arms above the elbows and led him out through a dim vaulted corridor and into the sudden vast space of the arena.

Yesterday the jeers of the crowd had given him the anger he needed to win.

Today the jeers were thin and empty as the soldiers prodded him into a lap of shame. Jonathan glanced up to his right. Those senators still in their seats were chatting or eating or studying slips of papyrus. Only a few bothered to curse him or throw rotten fruit. From one of the higher levels a lettuce drifted down and struck his naked shoulder. Other missiles landed harmlessly on the sand, now tinted pink by the high red awnings which filtered the noonday sun.

Jonathan's quick glance had shown him the looks of hatred on the few faces turned his way, so now he kept his head down as he continued his circuit of the arena. The feel of warm sand under the soles of his bare feet was familiar, but his feet themselves were not. He watched them move forward, first one foot, then the other. The left one was coated with blood, the right one only spattered. He knew they had put the blood on him to encourage some beast to devour him.

A masked figure with a mallet stood in the shadows and Jonathan shivered. If the beast didn't finish him, Pluto would.

Now, all too soon, he had completed his lap of dishonour. As the soldiers shoved Jonathan towards the centre of the arena he saw it for the first time: a cross on a hill.

He wondered if he was dreaming.

It must have been left from the morning beast fights: a sandy hillock with dwarf junipers and palms, and a false cave. On top of it stood a wooden cross and above the cross was a placard with the statement in red letters: I LAID A TORCH TO ROME.

This was no dream.

It was noon on the third day of the inaugural games of the magnificent new amphitheatre. The vela had been extended and in the rosy pink light the levels of the amphitheatre were swarming. Romans were moving about: buying snacks, unwrapping napkin lunches, going to the fountains for long drinks of wine-tinted water. Many seats were empty. Their occupants were placing bets on the upcoming gladiatorial shows, buying souvenir oil-lamps under the arches or even enjoying an hour at the new Baths of Titus, conveniently close to the amphitheatre.

This was the slack part of the day, between the bloody beast fights and the main gladiatorial combats. This was when common criminals were executed.

So only a few thousand people paid attention to the boy being paraded around the arena, its sand raked and fresh after the morning's hunt of hounds and beasts.

One or two senators – munching cheese and rye bread

in the lowest levels – commented on the admirable stoicism of the boy about to be executed.

'You see,' said one, gesturing with a piece of bread, 'these shows can be instructive. They show us that even the lower classes can die with dignity. Look how quietly he stands, allowing the soldiers to tie his wrists to the crossbar.'

The other nodded. 'But it's not over yet. Sometimes they don't really realise what's happening until the bear starts tearing at their flesh. That's the real test of bravery.'

'Vulture,' said the other. 'He's supposed to be re-enacting the death of Prometheus, so it'll be a vulture.'

'Can they train a vulture to peck a live person?'

'They trained that boar, the day before yesterday.'

'But they've smeared him with blood. Surely they only do that with carnivores.'

'Mmmm,' said the first one, popping the last bite of cheese in his mouth. 'I wonder what Pluto is saying to him?'

'It looks like he's just checking the ropes, to make sure they're tight. I'll wager ten sesterces the boy screams before the leopard touches him.'

'You're on,' said the other.

Lupus's teeth were chattering. His whole body had begun to shake as Jonathan was paraded around the vast arena. Now they were binding him to a cross and the water organ pumped a grim dirge. Lupus was about to see his best friend torn limb from limb by a wild beast. Could he watch? Could he not watch?

He glanced at Titus, and tried to hate him. But the

Emperor looked so miserable that he couldn't. Titus sat stiff and pale on his throne, and when Africanus leaned towards him as if to speak, the Emperor waved him away without taking his eyes from the arena.

Lupus looked for Nubia. But she had gone to the latrines nearly half an hour ago and had still not returned to her seat. She was probably hiding. He could not blame her. She hated blood.

Now, for the first time in three days, he also felt sick of it. This was a real person about to pour out his blood. Someone he loved like a brother. For a moment Lupus considered excusing himself and following Nubia's example. But it was already too late.

Below him an enormous black lion had just trotted into the arena.

'Dear gods!' whispered Africanus. 'A black lion! I thought they were the stuff of myth!'

'What?' asked Julia. 'What's special about a black lion?'

'They are fiercer and stronger than any other lion in the world,' said Africanus. 'When I was a little boy my nursemaid used to warn me that if I wasn't good the black lion would get me.'

Lupus felt an icy numbness. There was only one thing left for him to do. So he did it.

He closed his eyes and prayed.

Jonathan was struggling to free his hands from their bonds.

Pluto – the masked executioner – had not tightened them. Rather, he had loosened them and said: 'Run as fast as you can, out through the Gate of Death. I'll be waiting.' Pluto's voice had been familiar, and so had the small brown eyes gazing at him through the mask. But Jonathan couldn't place him. Terror had wiped his memory clean. 'Run as fast as you can.' Pluto had said.

But Pluto had not loosened them enough and Jonathan was still struggling to free his wrists.

He suddenly knew that he did not want to die. He wanted to live.

But the huge dark creature was almost upon him.

SCROLL XXXIII

The lion reared up and put heavy paws on Jonathan's shoulders.

Jonathan closed his eyes and waited for the end. He could smell the lion's fetid breath and he could hear it growling. And now he felt something hot and wet and rough on his chest. The lion was licking the blood off him! Any minute it would take a gigantic bite from him.

Jonathan finally wrenched his right hand free and was making a fist to strike the lion when a familiar voice called him from the cave, barely audible above the groaning chords of the water organ.

'Jonathan! It is the Monobaz. Don't hurt him and he will not hurt you.'

Nubia!

Jonathan opened his eyes to see the dark lion gazing back at him with blank golden eyes.

'It's Monobaz?' croaked Jonathan without moving his head. 'Are you sure?'

'Yes,' came her voice. 'We are disguising him with juice of walnut.'

Sure enough, Jonathan could now see that the golden fur on the lion's broad nose was streaked with some kind of brown dye.

'Scratch him behind the ear,' said an accented man's

voice, barely audible above the dramatic chords of the water organ. 'He likes that.'

Jonathan obediently scratched the lion behind the ear. The lion's growls grew louder. Suddenly Jonathan realised the lion wasn't growling. He was purring.

'Monobaz!' croaked Jonathan. 'Nice kitty.'

The deep ominous chords of the water organ faltered. Some people in the crowd were laughing. Others were cursing him or the lion.

Monobaz still rested heavy paws on Jonathan's shoulders, and as he continued to scratch Monobaz's ear, the big cat purred rhythmically.

'OW!' gasped Jonathan as Monobaz's sharp claws began to dig into his shoulders.

'Tell him "velvet paws!"' came the man's accented voice. 'He's just like a big kitten.'

'Velvet paws! Velvet paws!' cried Jonathan. The big cat obediently retracted his claws and dropped down on all fours. He began to lick the blood from Jonathan's legs and feet. The water organ was playing jolly music now and Jonathan heard the crowds laughing.

'Jonathan!' Nubia's voice from the cave. 'Get on his back!'

'What?' gasped Jonathan.

'I've been training him to let a person ride his back,' said Mnason. 'I'm almost certain he'll let you do it. Just say the word "Dionysus".'

Jonathan knew he had to act now or the moment would pass. Pluto had not sufficiently loosened the rope binding his left hand. It was still trapped. With a silent prayer he gave one strong wrench. It brought tears to his eyes but now his left hand was free. Without the rope holding him up his knees gave way and he nearly fell onto the lion. Somehow he managed to remain upright. He patted Monobaz on the head.

'Dionysus,' said Jonathan, but his voice came out as a croak. 'Dionysus!' he attempted again, and this time Monobaz seemed to react. The big cat stopped licking Jonathan's feet and stood quietly.

'Please God may this work,' muttered Jonathan. And then he climbed onto the back of the big black lion.

Lupus opened his tongueless mouth and cheered.

All around the amphitheatre people were laughing and cheering, too.

Jonathan had wrapped his arms round the lion's neck and his bare legs round its stomach. Now the beast and his rider moved slowly down the sandy hill, weaving through the palmettos until they reached the soft sand of the arena.

'By the gods!' said Titus. 'Look at that! I've never seen a person ride a man-eating lion before. Not even Carpophorus could do that.'

'The boy must be favoured by the gods!' gasped Africanus.

'The people think so, too,' said Calvus, nodding at the spectators. Lupus glanced away from Jonathan. The water organ was playing the deep triumphant tune it played whenever a gladiator won. Many people in the amphitheatre had their thumbs up. Others were waving white handkerchiefs. 'Mitte!' he heard them cry: 'Mitte!'

'They want you to spare him, pater!' Julia laughed.

'So they do,' said Titus, and Lupus heard him mutter,

'how fickle they are.'

Titus slowly rose from his throne and looked around at his subjects. Then he spread his arms wide and gave an exaggerated nod to show that he would bow to the wishes of the people and allow the boy to live.

The crowd went wild.

Lupus punched the air with his fist and added his cheer to the others.

And in the arena below him the black lion and his rider plodded steadily towards the Gate of Life.

'It seems the gods have spared you, Jonathan ben Morde-cai,' said the Emperor. 'I have never seen anything like that, a trained man-eater rubbing up against you like a big kitten ... I have pardoned you and you are free to go.'

In the Imperial Box, Jonathan knelt before Titus and bowed his head. 'Thank you, Caesar.'

Titus lifted Jonathan to his feet. The guards had found him an old red tunic and they had scrubbed most of the dried blood from the backs of his legs.

'Jonathan!' Nubia pushed between the guards and into the Imperial Box. 'You are alive!' She was feigning surprise but when she threw her arms around him and wept for joy he knew she was not pretending. Presently she let go of him and, catching sight of Lupus, she hugged him, too. They both turned and looked at Jonathan with eyes full of joy.

At that moment the bright notes of the trumpets blared and the deep chords of the water organ began the gladiator's march.

'Jonathan,' said Titus, 'I don't have long.' He gestured towards the gladiators entering the arena. 'You said the fire was an accident and I never gave you a chance to explain. Can you do so now? Quickly?'

Jonathan did so.

'I tried to stop him,' he said after he finished his account, 'but I failed. I'm sorry, Caesar. So sorry. All those people.'

The Emperor patted his shoulder. 'The gods have seen fit to pardon you and so do I. Go in peace, Jonathan ben Mordecai.' Even though the music was loud, Titus lowered his voice. 'And give your mother my love.'

Jonathan's head jerked up. 'My mother?' he said. He felt as if a cold hand had gripped his stomach and was squeezing it. 'She's dead. I ... my mother's dead. You attended her funeral. Didn't you?'

SCROLL XXXIV

'Dear gods,' said Titus. 'Don't you know? Of course you don't,' he turned away and then back. 'How could you?'

'Jonathan,' whispered Nubia. 'Your mother is alive. She is not dead.'

Jonathan stared at Nubia, whose eyes were full of tears. Then he looked at Lupus, who nodded vigorously and gave him a thumbs up. Out in the arena, the music soared.

'Her life was in danger ... as you know,' said the Emperor in a very low voice. 'We had to make it look as if she had died. Pretended to have a funeral. It was the only way to keep her safe. Do you understand?'

Jonathan nodded stupidly. He felt numb.

Suddenly a black barking shape exploded into the Imperial Box. Tigris hurled himself at Jonathan and covered his face with ecstatic kisses.

'By all the gods!' bellowed Titus, 'we can't have –'

'Jonathan!' cried Flavia Gemina, running into the box after Tigris. 'Are you free? Tigris ran out of the door and I followed him – oh, Jonathan!'

Flavia was hugging him tightly and Tigris was scrabbling at his legs with his paws.

'Ouch, Tigris!' gasped Jonathan, and to Flavia, 'Can't breathe!'

'Oh Jonathan, I'm sorry! I forgot about your asthma. Are you all right?'

'He's fine,' said Titus with a smile. 'He's just discovered that his mother is alive.'

'That's right, Jonathan!' cried Flavia. 'She and your father are together now. Together at home in Ostia. Oh, Jonathan! When they find out you're alive they'll be so happy!'

Jonathan nodded. He was glad to be holding a big squirming puppy in his arms. He didn't want them to see how much this news affected him.

'Now,' said Titus, 'I suggest that the four of you return to Ostia immediately.' He lowered his voice and leaned forward. 'There are many people in Rome who lost relatives in the fire. Today the people were for you, but they are a fickle lot. Tomorrow they may be against you. So go now. Quickly.'

Jonathan put down Tigris and followed his friends out of the box. But at the doorway he paused and looked back at Titus.

'Thank you, Caesar,' he said again.

Titus inclined his head and gave an odd half-smile. 'Shalom, Jonathan ben Mordecai. Peace be with you.'

'I can't believe I slept through all that,' Flavia said a short time later.

Jonathan nodded. He had been telling her about his escape from death as they walked back through the bright March afternoon to Senator Cornix's house.

At first the girls had put their arms round Jonathan's shoulders but he needed space to breathe and had shrugged them off. So now they walked four abreast with a big ecstatic puppy romping around them and getting tangled in their legs.

Jonathan was wheezing a little as they climbed the steep Clivus Scauri.

Suddenly Flavia stopped. 'How did you get free of the cross?'

'Yes,' said Nubia. 'Mnason and I could not think how to set you free without the people must see us.'

Jonathan stopped, too, and frowned. 'Oh no! I completely forgot. Pluto, the masked man. He loosened my ropes. He told me to run for the Gate of Death. I don't know who he was, though his voice sounded familiar.'

'Without him we could not save you. You would still be tied to cross.'

'I know. I owe him my life.'

Suddenly Tigris began to bark and they heard the sound of running footsteps behind them.

Jonathan's chest tightened with fear. They had come to drag him back to the amphitheatre. To do the job properly.

He turned and when he saw who it was he almost sobbed with relief.

Suddenly he knew.

'Here's my rescuer,' he said, unable to stop tears filling his eyes. 'Here's my Pluto.'

As the man came panting to a halt before them, Jonathan threw his arms around the big slave and hugged him.

'Caudex,' he said. 'Thank you.'

Nubia and her friends sat on padded seats in the dim

interior of a well-sprung carruca. They were on their way back to Ostia. Tigris lolled across Jonathan's lap, his eyes half closed, content to feel his master's hand on his head. Lupus sat on one side of Jonathan and Caudex on his other. Flavia was still weak, so she had stretched out along one whole bench with her head on Nubia's lap.

Beyond the canvas walls of the carruca and above the clip of the mules' hooves on stone and the grinding of the wheels, Nubia imagined she heard the faint roar of fifty thousand Romans cheering at the games.

She knew the gladiatorial combats were now underway. Would her brother be fighting? No, Taharqo had said he wouldn't fight for two more days. That meant he would be in his tent near the Golden House. She had not even thought to say goodbye to him.

Images passed through her mind. Taharqo running his victory lap around the arena. Taharqo pulling the green-eyed girl into his arms. Taharqo throwing back his head and laughing with white teeth. He might need her some day.

But he didn't need her today.

Nubia looked over at Jonathan. In the dim blue light of the covered carruca she saw that he gazed straight ahead, his battered fingers slowly moving on Tigris's head. She knew he was thinking of his mother.

Jonathan was the one who needed her. And Lupus, also unusually still and pensive. And Flavia, so deeply shaken by her ordeal in the water. Flavia must have felt Nubia's gaze because she turned her head a little and looked up. They smiled at each other.

Nubia stroked Flavia's light brown hair and felt a deep contentment as Flavia closed her eyes again.

Things would be good now. Their little family was reunited. She would look after them and make sure nothing ever separated them again. They had shared so many adventures. They had survived the volcano, the pirates, the assassins and the plague. And the games.

A huge surge of affection filled her as she looked at them.

Flavia, her eyes closed, breathing steadily.

Lupus, head down, deep in thought.

Jonathan, scratching Tigris behind his ear.

And brave Caudex, leaning back against one of the timber frames of the canvas roof, his eyes closed. He was part of their strange family, too. It occurred to Nubia that without Caudex they wouldn't be taking Jonathan home to his mother and father.

'Caudex?' she said softly.

'Yes?' Caudex opened his small brown eyes.

'How are you knowing they throw Jonathan to the beasts?'

Caudex shrugged his muscular shoulders. 'Flavia said people thought Jonathan started the fire. They throw those people to the lions. I told the man called Fabius that I would be Pluto.'

'Caudex, you're a hero,' murmured Flavia without opening her eyes.

Caudex grunted.

'And you were training to be a gladiator?' persisted Nubia.

Caudex nodded. 'Yes. Capua.'

Flavia opened her eyes. 'You're from Capua, too?'

Caudex shook his head. 'From Britannia. Trained in Capua.'

The cart rocked a little as it slipped out of a wheel rut.

'Why were you not becoming a gladiator?' asked Nubia.

'Don't like killing things. Hate blood.'

Nubia shook her head. 'Me too,' she said softly.

'How I got my name,' he said. 'Blockhead.'

'I always wondered why we called you that,' said Flavia, and to Nubia, 'Caudex means blockhead.'

'Why did they call you blockhead?' asked Nubia.

'Because I wouldn't kill a man.'

They all stared at him for a moment and then, almost apologetically, Lupus flapped his arms.

Nubia nodded solemnly. 'Lupus is right,' she said. 'You did kill someone. The man who plummets to earth. When you were being Pluto. You hit him on the head.'

'But Ganymede was dying,' said Flavia. 'Caudex was just putting him out of his misery.'

'Still, you killed him.'

They all looked at Jonathan in surprise. He had spoken for the first time since the carruca had rattled away from the Trigemina Gate. He was pulling Tigris's silky black ear between his thumb and forefinger.

'That must have been hard for you, Caudex,' said Jonathan quietly. 'Very hard.'

Caudex dropped his head. 'It was.'

'You did it for Jonathan, didn't you?' said Nubia.

Caudex nodded and looked up at them. 'I did it for all of you,' he said gruffly and looked around at them. 'You are like ... ' his voice trailed off. 'Family,' he said at last. 'You are like family.'

And as the carruca rolled on towards Ostia, Nubia smiled. She knew exactly what he meant.

THE LAST SCROLL

Sometime in the spring of AD 80 Titus opened a huge new amphitheatre with one hundred days of games. Now known as the Colosseum, the new amphitheatre was built with money and slave labour obtained by the conquest of Judaea ten years earlier. We know about Titus's games from several Latin authors, one of whom was actually present. Martial, as he is now known, was probably commissioned to write his *Book of the Spectacles* in order to glorify Titus.

Among the highlights mentioned by Martial are the parade of informers, the lion and the rabbit, the beast fighter Carpophorus, the female beast fighters, and the elaborately staged execution of criminals dressed as Orpheus, Laureolis, and Leander, the last of whom escaped his intended fate and was pardoned by Titus. We also know there were aquatic displays in the Colosseum, which means the complicated cells beneath the arena were not put in until later.

Gladiators from all over the Roman empire must have participated in Titus's games. Scholars believe they used Nero's Golden House as their base while the games were underway. (The Ludus Magnus gladiator school was not yet built).

Titus, Domitian, Domitia, Julia, Sabinus and Martial were all real. So were the two conspirators whom Titus invited to sit with him at the games, though we don't know their names. The rest of the characters in this book are fictional.

ARISTO'S SCROLL

Actaeon (*ak*-tay-on)
   mythological hunter who came upon the goddess Diana bathing; she turned him into a deer so that his own hounds pursued and devoured him

Aeneid (uh-*nee*-id)
   Virgil's epic poem about Aeneas, the hero whose descendants founded Rome

amphitheatre (*am*-fee-theatre)
   an oval-shaped stadium for watching gladiator shows, beast fights and executions; the Flavian amphitheatre in Rome (the 'Colosseum') is the most famous one

amphora (*am*-for-uh)
   large clay storage jar for holding wine, oil, grain, etc.

andabata (an-*da*-ba-ta)
   type of gladiator whose helmet had no eyeholes; he had to stab blindly at his opponent, usually another andabata

atrium (*eh*-tree-um)
   the reception room in larger Roman homes, often with skylight and pool

Aventine (*av*-en-tine)
   one of the seven hills of Rome, close to the River Tiber and Mount Testaccio

Baiae (*bye*-eye)
   a desirable area in the Bay of Naples where the richest people had villas

barbiton (*bar*-bi-ton)
   a kind of Greek bass lyre, but there is no evidence for a 'Syrian barbiton'

Berenice (bare-uh-*neece*)

a beautiful Jewish Queen who was Titus's lover after the sack of Jerusalem

Caelian (*kai*-lee-un)

one of the seven hills of Rome, site of the Temple of Claudius and many homes

Capitoline (*kap*-it-oh-line)

The Roman hill with the great Temple of Jupiter at its top; not as impressive today as it would have been in Flavia's time

Capua (*cap*-you-uh)

now known as Santa Maria Capua Vetere, 20 miles north of Naples, Capua was famous in Roman times for the gladiator school established by Julius Caesar

carruca (ka-*ru*-ka)

a four-wheeled travelling coach, often covered

Castor

one of the famous twins of Greek mythology (Pollux being the other)

ceramic (sir-*am*-ik)

clay which has been fired in a kiln, very hard and smooth.

Cerberus (*sir*-burr-uss)

three-headed mythological hellhound who guards the gates of the Underworld

Circus Maximus (*sir*-kuss *max*-i-muss)

long race-course in the centre of Rome, at the western foot of the Palatine Hill

Clivus Scauri (*klee*-vuss *scow*-ree)

a steep road on the Caelian Hill still visible today

Cloaca Maxima (klo-*ak*-ah *max*-im-ah)

the Great Drain: the sewer which ran under the Roman forum; it was so well-built that parts of it are still in use today

colonnade (coll-uh-*nayd*)

a covered walkway lined with columns

Colosseum (call-a-*see*-um)
    this nickname for the Flavian amphitheatre probably came
    from the colossal statue of Nero nearby; the term 'Colos-
    seum' was not used in Flavia's time
denarius (den-*are*-ee-us)
    small silver coin worth four sesterces
domina (*dom*-in-ah)
    a Latin word which means 'mistress'; a polite form of
    address for a woman
Daedalus (*die*-dal-uss)
    mythological inventor who was imprisoned by Minos of
    Crete; he made a maze called the labyrinth and also
    invented wings to escape his imprisonment
Dionysus (die-oh-*nye*-suss)
    Greek god of vineyards and wine; he is often shown riding
    a panther
Domitia (doh-*mish*-uh)
    Domitian's wife
Domitian (duh-*mish*-un)
    the Emperor Titus's younger brother, aged 30 when this
    story takes place
editor
    the person who sponsors (pays for) the games, in this case
    the Emperor Titus
Eurydice (your-*id*-iss-ee)
    in Greek mythology she was the beautiful wife of Orpheus
    who died of a snake bite; Orpheus went to the underworld
    to bring her back but did not succeed
ex machina (eks *mack*-ee-nah)
literally: 'from a crane'; usually referring to the part of a play
    where an actor dressed as a god or goddess is lowered onto
    the stage to put everything right.
familia (fam-*ill*-ya)
    the group of gladiators who train together in a particular

'school' are said to belong to one familia or 'family'

Flavia (*flay*-vee-a)

a name, meaning 'fair-haired'; Flavius is another form of this name

Flavian amphitheatre

what we know as the Colosseum; it was called Flavian because Vespasian, Titus and Domitian – who built it – were from the Flavian *gens* or tribe

forum (*for*-um)

ancient marketplace and civic centre in Roman towns

freedman (*freed*-man)

a slave who has been granted freedom, his ex-master becomes his patron

furca (*fur*-kah)

two-pronged fork used as an instrument of punishment, with two prongs to which the arms were tied; sometimes people were hung on it

furcifer (*fur*-kee-fare)

Latin for 'scoundrel'; literally someone who wears a forked piece of wood around their neck or who is crucified on a forked piece of wood

galerus (*gal*-air-uss)

the metal shoulder-guard of a retiarius; its large rim protected his head

gladiator / gladiatrix

refers to all classes of those who fought in the arena, but literally a man or woman who fights with a *gladius* (short thrusting sword)

greaves (*greevz*)

metal shin-guards; the Thracian and hoplomachus wore tall ones, the murmillo wore a single one on his left leg

habet! (*hab*-et)

Latin for 'he has!'; the crowds shouted this when a gladia-

tor received a hit; they also shouted hoc habet! 'he has it!'
(ie the hit or wound)

Hebrew (*hee*-brew)

holy language of the Old Testament, spoken by (religious)
Jews in the 1st century

hoplomachus (hop-lo-*mack*-uss)

type of gladiator armed like a Thracian with metal greaves
over quilted leg-guards and a brimmed helmet, but fought
with a round shield and short, straight sword

Ides (eyedz)

thirteenth day of most months in the Roman calendar
(including February); in March, July, October and May the
Ides occur on the fifteenth day of the month.

impluvium (im-*ploo*-vee-um)

a rainwater pool under a skylight in the atrium

Ionatano (yon-a-*tan*-oh)

the Latin alphabet had no 'J' and used the letter 'I' instead;
this is the dative case of Jonathan's name: 'to (or for)
Jonathan'

Isola Sacra (eye-sol-uh *sack*-ruh)

means 'sacred island'; a strip of land between Ostia's river
harbour and Claudius's new harbour to the north, its many
tombs can still be seen today.

iugula (*you*-gyoo-la)

the 'jugular vein', a major vein in the neck; crowds at the
amphitheatre shouted this if they wanted the victorious
gladiator to cut his defeated opponent's throat

Judaea (jew-*dee*-uh)

ancient province of the Roman Empire; modern Israel

Julia

the Emperor Titus's daughter, probably about fifteen
when this story takes place

Juno (*jew*-no)

queen of the Roman gods and wife of the god Jupiter

Jupiter (*jew*-pit-er)
> king of the Roman gods, husband of Juno and brother of Pluto and Neptune

kohl (*coal*)
> dark powder used to darken eyelids or outline eyes

lanista (la-*niss*-tuh)
> owner of a group of gladiators; he supervises their training and hires them out

lararium (lar-*ar*-ee-um)
> household shrine, often a chest with a miniature temple on top, sometimes a niche

Laureolus (low-ray-*oh*-luss)
> robber who was crucified and torn apart by beasts

Leander (lee-*and*-er)
> young man who swam across the Hellespont to meet his lover Hero, a beautiful priestess who signalled him from a tower; one night he drowned in a storm

libellus (lib-*ell*-uss)
> Latin for 'little book'; they contained statistics about the gladiators to help those who wanted to bet on the outcomes of gladiatorial combats

Ludus Aureus (*loo*-duss *ow*-ray-uss)
> before Domitian built the great Ludus Magnus, the gladiator school located in the Domus Aurea might have been known by this name

Ludus Dacicus (*loo*-duss *dak*-ee-kuss)
> one of the main gladiator schools in the first century AD

Ludus Gallicus (*loo*-duss *gall*-ik-uss)
> one of the main gladiator schools in the first century AD

Ludus Iulianus (*loo*-duss you-lee-*an*-uss)
> a famous gladiator school in Capua, founded by Julius Caesar

magister ludi (*mag*-iss-tur *loo*-dee)
> 'master of games'; the person in charge of organising the games

manica (*man*-ick-uh)
>   a gladiator's arm-guard, at this time in quilted linen or
>   leather, rarely metal

Martial (*marsh*-all)
>   Marcus Valerius Martialis; a poet of Spanish birth who
>   wrote a collection of of poems about the inaugural games
>   called 'de spectaculis'

medicus (*med*-ee-kuss)
>   the doctor at a gladiator school who looked after wounds
>   and patched men up

meta sudans (*met*-uh *su*-danz)
>   'sweaty turning post'; a famous conical fountain near the
>   Colosseum in Rome, it can no longer be seen

missio (*miss*-ee-oh)
>   Latin for 'I release'; the release granted to a defeated gladia-
>   tor to spare his life

mitte! (*mitt*-ay)
>   Latin for 'release!'; if the crowds think a defeated gladiator
>   fought well they shout this at the editor, hoping he will
>   allow the defeated gladiator to live

murmillo (mur-*mill*-oh)
>   type of gladiator who usually fought hoplomachus or
>   Thracian; he had a protected right arm and left leg, a big,
>   rectangular shield, brimmed helmet and short sword

Neapolis (nee-*ap*-o-liss)
>   a large city in the south of Italy near Vesuvius; modern Naples

Nereids (*near*-ee-idz)
>   mythological sea nymphs who were daughters of a wise
>   old sea god called Nereus

Nero (*near*-oh)
>   wicked Emperor who ruled Rome from AD 54 – AD 69

Oppian Hill (*opp*-ee-an)
>   part of the Esquiline Hill in Rome and site of Nero's
>   Golden House

Orpheus (*or*-fee-uss)

famous musician in Greek mythology; he played the lyre so beautifully that he charmed wild animals, rocks and even Cerberus when he went to the underworld to try to recover his beloved wife Eurydice (see above)

Ostia (*oss*-tee-uh)

port about 16 miles southwest of Rome; Ostia is Flavia's home town

Palatine (*pal*-uh-tine)

one of the seven hills of Rome; the greenest and most pleasant; the site of successive imperial palaces (the word 'palace' comes from 'Palatine')

palla (*pal*-uh)

a woman's cloak, could also be wrapped round the waist or worn over the head

palus (*pal*-uss)

wooden post used by gladiators to practice on

papyrus (puh-*pie*-russ)

the cheapest writing material, made of pounded Egyptian reeds

parma (*par*-ma)

small square shield used by the Thracian type gladiator

Pasiphae (*pass*-if-eye)

Mythological wife of Cretan king Minos who fell in love with a bull and later gave birth to the Minotaur, a creature with the body of a man and head of a bull

peristyle (*pare*-ri-style)

a columned walkway around an inner garden or courtyard

Persephone (purr-*sef*-fun-ee)

beautiful daughter of Demeter who was kidnapped by the god Pluto and reigns with him as queen of the underworld for six months out of the year

plebs

the ordinary people, the lowest class of freeborn Romans

Pliny (*plin*-ee)
> (the Elder) famous admiral and author who died in eruption of Vesuvius; his only surviving work is a *Natural History* in 37 chapters

Pluto (*ploo*-toe)
> god of the underworld, he is the Roman equivalent of Hades; in the games, a man may have dressed as Pluto to dispatch dying gladiators and criminals

Pollux
> one of the famous twins of Greek mythology (Castor being the other)

pontifex maximus
> literally: the greatest priest; this term is still applied to the Pope in Rome

Potsherd Mountain
> now known as Mount Testaccio, this hill was made of millions of sherds of broken oil amphoras methodically discarded behind the river warehouses

retiarius (ret-ee-*are*-ee-uss)
> type of gladiator who usually fought secutor; he wore manica and galerus on his left arm and fought with net, trident and dagger; his name means 'net-man'

Sabinus (sa-*bee*-nuss)
> Titus Flavius Sabinus; husband (and cousin) of Titus's daughter Julia

scroll (skrole)
> a papyrus or parchment 'book', unrolled from side to side as it was read

secutor (*seck*-you-tor)
> type of gladiator who usually fought retiarius; armed like a murmillo but his smooth tight helmet enclosed the head completely, apart from small eyeholes

Seneca (*sen*-eh-kuh)
> Nero's tutor and Stoic philosopher who wrote about how

to die a good death

sesterces (sess-*tur*-sees)
more than one *sestertius*, a brass coin; four sesterces equal a denarius

shalom (shah-*lome*)
the Hebrew word for 'peace'; can also mean 'hello' or 'goodbye'

sica (*seek*-uh)
sickle-shaped dagger used by Jewish assassins in the first century AD

Spartacus (*spar*-tuh-kuss)
famous gladiator from Thrace who escaped from the training school at Capua to lead 6,000 slaves on a revolt which lasted two years before being quelled

Stagnum (*stag*-num)
artificial lake across the Tiber river; built by Augustus, it was used during the inaugural games of the Colosseum for mock sea battles

stibium (*stib*-ee-um)
powder used by women in Roman times to colour their eyelids

Stoic (*stow*-ick)
a Greek philosophy popular in ancient Rome; its followers admired moral virtue, self-discipline and indifference to pleasure or pain.

stola (*stole*-uh)
a long tunic worn mostly by Roman matrons (married women)

stylus (*stile*-us)
a metal, wood or ivory tool for writing on wax tablets

tac! (tak)
a shortened form of the Latin imperative 'tace' ('be quiet')

Tarpeian (tar-*pay*-un)
a cliff on the Capitoline Hill; traitors were executed by being thrown off it

Tartarus (*tar*-tar-uss)

the underworld or land of the dead ruled by Pluto, who is sometimes known as Tartarus

Thetis (*thet*-iss)

beautiful Nereid (sea-nymph) who was the mother of Achilles

Thrace (*thrace*)

region of Northern Greece which became a Roman province about 40 years before this story takes place

Thracian (*thrace*-shun)

gladiator armed like a hoplomachus with metal greaves over quilted leg-guards and a brimmed helmet, but fought with a small, square shield and curved sword

tiro (*teer*-oh)

novice gladiator who has never fought in the arena or is fighting for the first time

Titus (*tie*-tuss)

Titus Flavius Vespasianus, 40 year old son of Vespasian, has been Emperor of Rome for nine months when this story takes place.

toga (*toe*-ga)

a blanket-like outer garment, worn by freeborn men and boys

Torah (*tor*-uh)

Hebrew word meaning 'law' or 'instruction'. It can refer to the first five books of the Bible or to the entire Hebrew scriptures

triclinium (trick-*lin*-ee-um)

ancient Roman dining room, usually with three couches to recline on

Trigemina Gate (try-*gem*-in-ah gate)

gate with three arches which led from Rome to the via Ostiensis

trigon (*try*-gon)

ball game where three players stand at different points of an imaginary triangle and throw a ball to each other as fast and hard as they can; you lose if you drop it

tunic (*tew*-nic)

a piece of clothing like a big T-shirt; children often wore a long-sleeved one

vela (*vel*-uh)

awnings or sails; there were massive vela on masts above the new amphitheatre (Colosseum) to provide shade for the people

venator (ven-*ah*-tor)

Latin for hunter; these were the skilled men who fought in the beast fights

venatrix (ven-*ah*-tricks)

a female beast-fighter

Vespasian (vess-*pay*-zhun)

Roman Emperor who died nine months before this story begins; Titus's father

Vesuvius (vuh-*soo*-vee-yus)

the volcano near Naples which erupted on 24 August AD 79

Virgil (*vur*-jill)

a famous Latin poet who lived about 100 years before this story takes place

wax tablet

a wax-covered rectangle of wood used for making notes

——— The Roman Mysteries ———

I   THE THIEVES OF OSTIA

In the bustling, cosmopolitan port of Ostia, near Rome, a killer is at large. He is trying to silence the watchdogs. Flavia Gemina and her three new friends – Jonathan, Lupus and Nubia – follow the trail to find out why.

II   THE SECRETS OF VESUVIUS

The four friends are staying near Pompeii, and trying to solve a strange riddle, when Mount Vesuvius erupts and they must flee for their lives. A thrilling account of one of the greatest natural disasters of all time.

III   THE PIRATES OF POMPEII

The four friends discover that children are being kidnapped from the camps where hundreds of refugees are sheltering after the eruption of Vesuvius, and proceed to solve the mystery of the pirates of Pompeii.

IV   THE ASSASSINS OF ROME

Jonathan disappears and his friends trace him to the Golden House of the Emperor Nero in Rome, where they learn the terrible story of what happened to his family in Jerusalem – and face a deadly assassin.

V THE DOLPHINS OF LAURENTUM

Off the coast of Laurentum, near Ostia, is a sunken wreck full of treasure. The friends are determined to retrieve it – but so is someone else. An exciting adventure which reveals the secret of Lupus's past.

VI THE TWELVE TASKS OF FLAVIA GEMINA

It's December AD 79, and time for the Saturnalia festival, when anything goes. There's a lion on the loose in Ostia – and Flavia has reason to suspect the motives of a Roman widow who is interested in her father.

VII THE ENEMIES OF JUPITER

Emperor Titus summons the children to help him find the mysterious enemy who seeks to destroy Rome through plague and fire. Jonathan is distracted by a secret mission of his own, and suddenly everything gets terrifyingly out of control.

VIII THE GLADIATORS FROM CAPUA

IX THE COLOSSUS OF RHODES
coming shortly!